Published by Familius LLC, www.familius.com
Familius books are available at special discounts for bulk purchases
for sales promotions or for family or corporate use. Special edi-
tions, including personalized covers, excerpts of existing books, or
books with corporate logos, can be created in large quantities for
special needs. For more information, contact Premium Sales at
559-876-2170 or email specialmarkets@familius.com.

Library of Congress Catalog-in-Publication Data
2015940079

Hardcover ISBN 9781942934059
E-book ISBN 9781942934202

Printed in the United States of America

Edited by Lindsay Sandberg
Cover design by David Miles
Book design by Brooke Jorden

10 9 8 7 6 5 4 3 2 1

First Edition

CHRISTMAS WONDERS

ROBYN BUTTARS

Dedicated to my siblings—Montana, Blake, Crystal, and Tad—who shared the Christmas Wonders of my youth, and in appreciation to Barbara Hales and Rick Walton for endorsing great stories.

CHAPTER ONE

Cradled in his mother's arms, Luke nestled against her body as the steady rhythm of her unlabored breathing lulled him into a reservoir of serenity. Rocking from side to side, she began to hum. He was falling into a peaceful twilight—almost sleep. But Luke, unwilling to rest with her near, forced himself to stir from the tender cocoon so he could gaze into her face.

She touched his cheek. Her fingers lingered near his lips as though waiting for them to curl up in recognition. Then she smiled. It was not the tentative response of her fragile, weary body that still glowed in his mind's eye. This smile was not the one he remembered. No longer earthbound, it flamed with the soul-blazing brilliance of an angel.

"Luke." Someone shook him.

"Mother!" Luke cried. He refused to wake up—not yet!

"Don't go." His helpless plea echoed off bare walls as she faded into the recesses of his memory.

"It's just a dream." Dad's brusque voice sliced through Luke. "Come on. You need to get dressed."

Luke turned away from the demand. With eyes closed, he attempted to fade back into the dream, to spend another blessed moment with her.

"Get up." Dad pulled him to the edge of the bed. "Now!"

His mother was gone.

Luke sat up and shifted his legs to the floor. His shoulders sagged as he reached down to retrieve the pants crumpled at the side of the bed.

"You can't wear those." Dad stepped into the hall. With a flick of his hand, he motioned to the row of boxes. "Find some clean clothes for school."

Luke jumped to his feet. "School? What do you mean?"

Without answering, Dad walked through the doorway that joined the apartment to the cobbler shop. He didn't bother to shut the door behind him.

Luke trudged from his room. Last night their new neighbor said something about school, but he hadn't connected it with his reality. He opened the first box. An Evans Bank calendar covered the kitchen utensils. *Always here to help our neighbors* was printed in fancy, red lettering below the 1965. He pushed the cardboard flaps closed and slowly opened the next box. If he dawdled long enough, maybe Dad would forget about him, or at least forget about school. Everything stable had crumbled in his life. How could he face the newness of his existence?

"Luke, hurry up!" Dad's voice pierced the silence.

He opened two more boxes and gave them a cursory glance. In the fifth box, he found a wrinkled shirt and jeans.

"Luuuuuke."

Luke ran back to the side of his bed, grabbed the socks off the floor, yanked them on, and slipped his feet into his heavy brown boots. With laces untied, he stumbled toward the cobbler shop.

"Be on your way, now," Dad said.

"Umm . . . where is it?"

"We passed it on the way in last night." Dad nodded in the direction they had come. "It's a red building, just a couple of blocks."

Luke didn't move.

"Well?" Dad said, turning to face him.

"Won't you come with me?" Luke pulled at the loose thread on his sleeve.

"I have work to do." Dad shook his head and turned back to the cobbler's bench.

Luke walked to the door, pulled it open, and stepped out into the late September morning. He glanced both ways down the street. The town was quiet. There were just a few cars parked on the narrow road and only two people walking on the sidewalk.

Across the street, colored lights on Nan's Diner blinked

off and on randomly. They looked out of place in the bright sun. Luke stepped to the edge of the curb and waited for a car to pass before crossing. In the display window of Nan's Diner was a tray of cinnamon rolls slathered with white frosting. Luke recalled Nan's comment about her "award winning" rolls.

Last night, after driving all day to get to the city, he and Dad were unloading the pickup when Nan crossed the street with a sack in her hand. She waved at Luke when she caught his eye. He turned away, pretending he didn't see her as he lugged a heavy box to the door of the shop.

She followed him inside. "Welcome to the neighborhood," she called in a cheerful voice.

Luke flipped around and sniffed the air like a hungry puppy.

"I'm Nan from across the street. And you are?"

"Ma'am." Dad stepped toward her. "I'm Jeffrey, and this is Luke."

"Well, it's sure good to meet you both. Merv's arthritis is really getting to him, so we need a good cobbler around—"

"I just repair boots, ma'am," Dad interjected. "Someone had to at the ranch, but . . ." He glanced at the row of women's shoes.

"Don't worry about those. Merv can tell you how to do the easy stuff." Nan set her sack on the counter. "I brought you some leftovers from my diner—something to fill your stomachs while you get settled."

"Mighty obliged." Dad's eyes rested on the package.

"Wish I could stay and help, but I'm a man short on the cleanup crew tonight." She crossed the room, disappearing as quickly as she appeared.

If Nan had left then Dad probably wouldn't have thought about school, but she turned around just outside the door and poked her head back in. Her clear green eyes surveyed Luke from head to toe. "How old are you?"

Luke put his shoulders back and lifted his head. "Nine."

"Fourth grade." She looked at Dad. "School starts at 8:30." With a quick smile in Luke's direction, she said, "Stop by the diner and I'll give you one of my prizewinning cinnamon rolls."

Dad opened her package before she made it to the street. He pulled out two take-home boxes filled with heaps of potatoes flooded with deep brown gravy, stacks of roast beef, and piles of green beans.

———

Plump, juicy raisins broke through the frosting on one of the trays of cinnamon rolls. Luke's stomach growled; he hadn't thought to grab something for breakfast. He put his hand on the door to the diner before pulling it back. Longingly, Luke looked at the cinnamon rolls, but he didn't go inside. Instead he turned away, forcing his feet to continue down the sidewalk. At the corner, he veered left in a reverse of their entrance into town.

A woman waved to him from inside the window of the

drugstore. He nodded, and then brought his head back into a straight line with the cement, hoping he was headed in the right direction. Dad hadn't mentioned the school when they drove into the city. That wasn't surprising because Dad hadn't said anything at all until they pulled up in front of the cobbler shop. With a sigh, he had taken his cap off and trailed his fingers through his sandy hair.

"This is it." He rested his head on the steering wheel for one brief moment, and then plopped the cap back on his head and opened the door of the pickup.

A yellow bus passed Luke on the street and someone yelled, "Hey boy."

Luke watched the bus until it turned off the road. When he reached the turnoff, he stopped and stared at the two-story red brick building. Although it didn't look menacing, it didn't look inviting either. Boys and girls strolled toward the building and a group of little boys chased a big boy holding a brown, paper bag above his head. Their screams punctuated his anxiety. After taking a deep breath, he slapped at the knot lodged inside his chest and attempted to swallow it. With clenched fists, he turned onto the sidewalk leading to a wide row of cement stairs.

Halfway up the steps, a girl in a yellow dress, who was walking just ahead of him, stopped. Her curious glance traveled over his shirt and pants before resting on his scuffed brown boots with the loose laces.

Two missing teeth left a big gap in her grin. "You're new," she said, staring into his eyes.

Luke nodded.

"Who's your teacher?"

He shrugged.

The girl led the way up the steps and held the school door open for him. "There's the office." She pointed at an open doorway.

"Thanks." He stepped into a cavernous hall.

Children rushed past him, their boisterous voices bouncing off the tiles. A boy bumped into him, called out a hurried apology, and scurried on his way. Luke put his head down and made a beeline to the office. Inside, he glanced past the empty, wooden chairs before looking at a woman on the other side of a counter. Her back was toward him.

As though she sensed his presence, she turned around, her eyes skimmed across his face before returning to the papers in her hand. "May I help you?"

"Umm." Luke tried to answer but didn't know what to say.

She leaned across the counter. "Are you looking for someone . . . visiting . . . new student—?"

He tilted his head forward before she could list another option.

"Oh!" Her eyes settled on his face momentarily while she reached under the counter and grabbed a notebook and pen. "Welcome. What's your name?"

"Luke."

"Last name?"

"Cardston."

She wrote on her paper and fired another question. "Where do you live?"

"Behind the cobbler shop."

"I mean your address," she said, her voice sharp.

"I . . . I don't know."

The woman looked up from the notebook and her face softened, her lips tipped into a slight smile. "Don't worry about this," she said, closing the notebook. "It's just for my information. Your folks will fill in the details." She turned to a filing cabinet and pulled out a small stack of papers before walking around the counter. After a quick glance through the waiting room, she stepped to the office door and looked toward the front of the school. "Is your mom here?"

Luke dropped his eyes to the scuffed boots. "No, ma'am."

She walked over to him and tapped her fingers on the counter. "Your dad?"

He pursed his lips together. She sounded irritated. "No, ma'am," he said politely.

The tapping stopped. She gawked at him, mouth hanging open. "You're alone? You've got to be . . ." After drawing in a jagged breath, she pushed the air out between clenched teeth.

Luke couldn't hear what she muttered.

With a wave of her hand she turned from him. "Come with me. Principal Ashton will have to help you."

Luke followed her down a narrow hall until they reached a closed door.

"There's a magazine." She pointed to a table between two chairs. "Principal Ashton may be a while."

Luke sat back on one of the chairs, dangling his legs over the thick wooden seat. From his perch he could see two other closed doors and one large, framed picture of the sun shining through a red, rock arch. When he got tired of staring at the picture, he stood and sifted through the magazines on the table, barely noticing the covers until—his hand trembled as he pulled out a magazine with a picture of Astronaut White and the worldview from the spacewalk. His heart raced. He and Grandpa had read it together.

Without warning, tears brimmed in Luke's eyes. Grandpa was gone. He only lived a day after the Black Angus bull caught him in the corner of the corral. The magazine—Luke's final tribute—and a few wild flowers were the only remembrances on the homemade, wooden casket as it was lowered into the rocky earth.

Two months later, Dad left Luke at the ranch to do the evening chores while he went into town. Luke waited for his return until long after dark, but finally fell asleep in the big, wooden rocking chair. When he awoke the next morning, Dad was on the floor by the fireplace.

"Dad?" Luke put his hand to Dad's cheek.

"Hmm?" Dad bolted upright. "What's . . . ?" He glanced at Luke, then slumped over, buried his face in his hands and groaned.

Luke fell to his knees beside him and touched his

shoulder. "Dad?" The sound was a forced whisper. "Dad," he said louder, covering Dad's large, weathered hands with his own.

In one fluid movement, Dad stood and walked across the room. Pausing at the door, he glanced back at Luke. "Start packing," he said, "we're moving."

"Moving?" The simple word was as foreign to Luke as the Italian arias on Grandpa's 45 RPM records.

Dad grabbed his cowboy hat off the nail by the door. "The bank's foreclosing on the ranch." He jammed the hat onto his head, but his voice didn't even break as he pronounced their sentence.

They loaded their possessions in the pickup, covered them with a tarp, and drove away from the only life Luke had known. Two of the old cowboys waved as they bounced down the dirt road, stirring up clouds of dust. Luke looked back to set the memory of home in his mind, but the dust cloud was like a veil covering all that was familiar. Ahead was something he couldn't even imagine.

CHAPTER TWO

Hushed voices drifted down the quiet hall from the front office. When Luke's name was spoken, he sat up straighter, trying to tune into the conversation, but the words were too muffled to understand.

He opened the magazine, glanced at the pictures, and started to read the article about the true space adventure. The familiar sentences wrapped around him like the comforting promise of home after a long journey. Inhaling deeply, he relaxed his shoulders. Air escaped slowly through his mouth.

"He's alone?" A man's deep voice preceded him from the office to the hall. The man stopped in front of Luke, introduced himself, and glanced at the open magazine in Luke's lap. "That's a great article. Have you read it?"

"Yes, sir."

"Bring it in my office. I'd like to hear you read."

They sat together in front of a cluttered desk and Luke began to read. After a few paragraphs, Principal Ashton put his hand on Luke's arm. His smile chased away the wrinkles that made him look so stern. "Very good." He looked at his watch. "I need to talk to your dad. Do you think he's home?"

Luke shook his head. "He's at the shop."

"Come with me, son." He stood and walked to the door, pulled a hat off the coat rack and settled it lightly on his head.

———

The old, brass bell jingled when Luke opened the door to the cobbler shop.

Dad's flash of anger charged across the room. "Why are you—?" His eyes shifted to Principal Ashton.

Principal Ashton glanced around the shop before looking directly at the workbench where Dad sat. "Mr. Cardston?" He stepped next to Luke.

Dad nodded.

"I'm Principal Ashton." He put his hand on Luke's shoulder. "Is this your son?"

"Uh huh." Dad pushed his stool away from the workbench.

"Why didn't you bring him to school?" Principal Ashton's question hovered in the room like an accusation.

Dad stood, meeting the principal's eyes on his own level. "I'm busy."

"So am I," Principal Ashton replied. "We can't admit him without your cooperation. You have to sign papers. We need his past school records—"

Dad put his hand up as though determined to stop the flow of demands. "He hasn't been to school."

Principal Ashton glanced at Luke. "Why?"

"We lived on a mountain ranch. It was fifty miles down an unpaved—"

"Where did he learn to read so well?"

"His grandpa taught him the basics and they read his mother's books." Dad stretched up to the shelf at his side, jiggled the end of a mallet, and pulled it into his hand.

Principal Ashton turned to Luke. When their eyes met, he sighed. "His mother?"

Dad bounced the mallet in his hands before easing himself back onto his bench. "Died five years ago," he said.

Principal Ashton walked over to the table. "You'll have to come to the school so we can register Luke."

Dad flicked his head up, just enough to see where Principal Ashton stood. "I'll come during lunch."

"No." Principal Ashton's abrupt laugh held no humor. "Come now."

━━━━━━━━━

Luke seemed distracted while Dad and Principal Ashton discussed details of registration, but as they walked down the hall toward his classroom, he gazed at the long row of narrow, metal doors and the bulletin boards with bright, fall pictures. When a door flew open at his side, he stopped and stared at the group of students who ran out of the room carrying balls, ropes, or small tied bags.

After being introduced, his teacher, Mrs. Layne, put her hand on his shoulder and looked into his face. "Glad to have you in our class, Luke," she said and then introduced him to the other students. Beckoning for him to follow her, she led him to a desk in the far corner of the room. The principal directed Dad to take a seat along the wall behind him.

Mrs. Layne passed a worksheet down the rows and then returned to Luke. She asked a few questions concerning where he came from, what he liked to do, and what his favorite subjects were. Luke seemed confused by the questions and it wasn't long before Dad stepped to his side and explained this was his first time in school.

"Oh," she said, her eyes settling on Luke's face as though seeing him for the first time. "Umm . . . well, let's see what you can do with the worksheet." She set a paper on his desk along with two sharpened pencils.

Luke answered the simple addition and subtraction equations until he came to a problem he didn't understand. He turned to ask his dad for help. Dad was gone. Luke set the pencil down and looked straight ahead.

It wasn't long before Mrs. Layne walked by and glanced at his paper. "I'll be teaching you how to do these." She pointed to the rows of empty spaces then turned to the class. "As soon as you have completed the worksheet, you may go out for a fifteen minute recess."

Luke stayed in his seat until everyone left the room except Mrs. Layne and a girl in a wheelchair.

"Grace wants to go outside. Would you please push her?" Mrs. Layne asked, tilting her head toward the girl in the wheelchair.

Luke stepped behind Grace and pushed her out the door.

"Take me over there." Grace pointed to two lines of students on the grass. "You can play dodgeball with them."

As they approached the students Grace yelled, "Let Luke in."

One of the girls moved over, pointing out the place for him to stand.

"What do I do?"

"Don't let the ball hit you." She leaned over, set her hands on her knees, and stared at the opposing students.

The boy on the other side threw the ball directly at Luke. Having been raised in the mountains where alert eyes and quick responses were necessary to keep one from danger, Luke followed his instincts, avoiding the hit. One by one, students left the game until he was one of two still standing on his team.

"There's Mrs. Layne. Recess is over," Grace called pushing herself toward the school.

Luke ran to catch up with her.

"Thanks." Grace folded her hands in her lap.

Luke pushed her across the schoolyard until they reached Mrs. Layne. Their teacher smiled at Luke and reached out to take control of the wheelchair.

"I can do it, ma'am." He pushed Grace up the steep ramp, into the school, and over to her own desk.

The rest of the day dragged on forever. Being cooped up in a room with no freedom to move about was almost more than Luke could handle. The steady, regimented flow of unfamiliar work caused him to fidget like a calf picking up the scent of a cougar. It wasn't until the end of the day that Luke seemed to take an interest.

Mrs. Layne sat at the front of the room and held up a book. "Please clear off your desks," she instructed. "We have time to read a chapter."

Some of the boys moaned and glanced at each other with meaningful nods. Luke leaned forward, his elbow on the desk, chin resting on his hand. Mrs. Layne read from a book he recognized; there was a copy in his mother's collection. He and Grandpa had spent many hours reading it together.

He listened attentively as his teacher's voice skipped lightly over the unforgettable phrases. Soon he was wrapped in the words, the story, and the memory of the warm, cabin fireplace on a cold winter day.

Mrs. Layne read only a few pages before the noisy antics of some of the boys distracted her. She stopped; her glance quieted them enough for her to continue. As soon as she started reading, the boys resumed their challenge. She turned the page and stopped again. This time she glared at the offending boys.

"Shhhh," Luke demanded the third time she stopped.

Mrs. Layne didn't have to stop reading again until the bell rang. "Spelling test tomorrow," she said, closing the book.

The other students were out of the room before Luke realized his first school day was over. Following their lead, he walked to the door and then stepped to the side, allowing a woman to enter the room.

"Hi, Mom." Grace wheeled herself toward the door. "This is Luke, my new friend."

The woman smiled. "That's great!" Her eyes sparkled with dancing light.

He nodded at the woman on his way out of the room. "Friend?" Luke said the word to himself a few times, as though he were trying to figure out what it meant. The look of concentration remained on his face all the way down the hall and out of the school.

CHAPTER THREE

Life fell into a patterned continuation of days. Five days a week, Luke went to school. On the weekends, he stayed in the apartment or explored a small area around his new home. October came and went without much of a change, not even for Halloween. Although kids at school talked about their costumes and activities, his day was like any other, except for two noticeable differences. Merv, the man who owned the cobbler shop, shoe store, and their apartment, gave him a handful of trick-or-treat candy, and Carma, the woman who owned the bookstore, invited him to join her for a donut and cup of hot chocolate.

It wasn't until a couple of weeks into November that Luke's feeling of being the new kid began to ease. He tried hard to fit in, and as he got used to the work and school routine, he was more secure in his surroundings. However, his loneliness increased as Thanksgiving drew near.

That one holiday was always celebrated on the ranch. Grandpa said it didn't matter if their women folk were gone; they still needed to be grateful. He cooked up a wild turkey and a big roast with all the trimmings, put the extra leaves in the table, and invited the cowboys who had helped since the spring cattle branding to join them. Occasionally, one of the younger cowboys had a special girl to bring along. Usually it was just a table full of hungry men who broke away from work to share a prayer of gratitude and a hearty meal.

The season sharpened Luke's memories of Grandpa and the ranch. Without Grandpa, there would be no reason to set the table, no turkey, no celebration. However, when he walked by Nan's Diner a week before Thanksgiving, his outlook changed when he bumped into Nan.

She laughed a startled trill and reached for his arm. "This is good timing. I was just thinking about you."

"You were?"

Nan gave one fast nod. "I hope you and your dad are planning on Thanksgiving dinner with us."

Luke stepped back, eyes wide, his breath bottled in his chest. Thanksgiving with Nan—was that possible?

"Umm . . . I don't." He shrugged. "My dad—"

"I was just on my way to tell him what time we'll be eating." Nan winked at Luke and grinned.

Perhaps Dad wouldn't have a chance to refuse. Luke pushed the door to the cobbler shop open and waited for Nan to go in front of him.

"Jeffrey," she said, two steps from the door, "We're planning on you and Luke for Thanksgiving dinner—twelve o'clock sharp."

———

On Thanksgiving morning, Luke awoke early with a sense of excitement he hadn't known for a year. Dad didn't say anything about going to Nan's the night before, but that didn't stop the holiday feeling that settled over the town and reached into his own heart. Luke jumped out of bed and ran through the shop to the front window. There wasn't a car or person in sight and all was quiet, yet it didn't feel deserted, just safely on hold for the special day.

"What are you doing?"

Luke jumped and flipped around. Dad leaned over the sewing machine in the corner.

"Ju-just looking," he stammered. "Happy Thanksgiving."

"Hmmm." Dad's eyes returned to his project before Luke finished his Thanksgiving greeting.

Luke wandered back into the apartment, rolled a left-over pancake like a scroll, and slumped into the rocking chair. Eyes closed, he rested his head while taking bites in rhythm to the squeaking rockers. Dad was working. Still, it was Thanksgiving. He swallowed the last bite of pancake on his way to the stack of boxes. After finding the shirt and slacks he wore to Grandpa's memorial service, he dressed, brushed his teeth, and slicked down his cowlick with Dad's hair gel. Ready with nowhere to go, he grabbed a book and settled into the rocking chair, seeming determined to believe that immersing himself in a good story would be holiday enough.

Just before noon, someone knocked on the cobber shop door. Luke lurched forward, but then dropped back in the chair. Dad would handle it himself. Leaning toward the door that divided the apartment from the shop, he tipped his head to listen for footsteps. Nothing. A few seconds passed—another knock, louder than before.

He remained seated, but his feet bounced. Barely restraining himself from running to the door, he listened, waiting for Dad to acknowledge the person standing outside. Silence. Forcing his mind to return to his book, Luke read several sentences before a loud pounding on the front door startled him. He jumped. The book fell to the floor.

"I'm coming." Dad's voice was tight with control.

Luke ran into the shop. Dad unlocked the door and pulled it open.

Merv released a laugh that projected into the room with his excited greeting. "Oh, you're here! Thought you were still asleep when you didn't answer and I couldn't let you miss Nan's dinner. Let's go over together. I hate to walk in there alone . . ." He turned toward Luke with an approving nod and then glanced at his watch. "We better—"

"Sorry," Dad interrupted as he turned away from the door. "We're not . . ." His words trailed to a stop when he saw Luke.

Merv stepped into the shop and closed the door behind him. "Nan invited you, didn't she?"

"Yes, but—"

"My friend, I'd suggest you change your mind unless you want to have Thanksgiving dinner here." Merv held out both hands and turned to include every corner of the small shop. "It'd be pretty hard to seat all her guests in this little area." He glanced at Luke and winked. "And your apartment isn't big enough to hold half of them."

"Huh?" Dad planted his feet and glared at Merv.

"I lived in that little apartment for a couple years. The first year Nan invited me for Thanksgiving, I didn't want to go. So I didn't." He shook his head and chuckled. "About 12:30, there was a knock on this door—Nan and her guests, arms full of the Thanksgiving feast. We ate here. The table for Nan's parents was right over in that corner." He pointed to the small counter by the sewing machine. "Nan and her cook sat at my work table, and me and . . . oh, I can't remember her name." He shrugged. "We stood, trying to balance our plates on the window sill.

"There were only six of us that Thanksgiving. But now? She probably has twelve, maybe fifteen guests. Where you going to put that many people and all that food?" Merv's eyes danced with laughter but no sound escaped from his mouth.

Dad turned to the right and then to the left, his eyes lighting on each spot Merv described. "She wouldn't." His mouth drew down into a solid frown as he shook his head.

"No?" Merv laughed. "How well do you know Nan?"

Dad shrugged. "I've talked to her a couple of times."

"She's one of the most determined women you'll ever meet. If she's invited you," he said, pointing at Dad, "she plans on you." He turned to Luke. "Do you want to go with me or wait for your dad?"

Luke waited.

After Dad changed his clothes, Luke ran to keep up with his long steps as they crossed the street. When Dad opened the door, the smell of roasted meat and freshly baked pies wafted through the air in a mouth-watering invitation.

They paused long enough to take a quick look around the diner. Long, fluorescent bulbs outlined the high ceiling and cast shadows over yellowed walls. When Dad started down the aisle, Luke followed between the brown benches and a soda fountain with high, vinyl-covered stools. He pushed one; it moved. With a firm hand, he set the remaining stools spinning. His merry eyes reflected the dim lights on the wall-length mirror.

At the far end of the room, they entered a short hall that led to a dining area. Metal sconces, electric candles aglow, hung on the walls. Long tables were covered with white tablecloths, silverware, and matching flowered plates.

Merv flipped his thumb up when he caught Luke's eye. With a shift of his hand, he pointed at two chairs across the table from where he was seated. Luke pressed in behind Dad, nodding in return to the welcoming comments from those they passed.

After slipping into his chair, Luke glanced around the room, recognizing some of the guests from his explorations along the street. His stomach growled, but nobody could hear it above the low roar of festive chatter.

Nan finally came in, looking a bit frazzled in her white apron, but smiling as though she were having the time of her life. "Welcome," she said. Everyone quieted down.

"For those of you who don't know, these are my parents." Her hands rested on the shoulders of a man and woman seated in the middle of the table. "Now, let's go around the table so you can introduce yourselves."

One by one, the people in the room stood and said their name. Some added a comment about Thanksgiving, being together, or the delicious smells in the air. Merv thanked Nan for "getting a crowd together."

Luke's eyes shifted between Dad and those who were left to introduce themselves. Two people, then one. If he didn't stand, Dad would handle introductions himself. As Dad pushed his chair away from the table, Luke jumped up.

"I like Thanksgiving," he blurted, then plopped back on his chair.

His comment was so quick that Dad didn't even have

to pause after standing. Dad glared at Luke, his eyebrows drawn together by his frown. He glanced down the rows of guests. "I'm Jeffrey." He nodded toward Luke. "Luke."

The woman who worked at the corner drugstore was the last person to stand. "Hi, everyone." She smiled. Her eyes lit on each person around the table. "I'm Donna and I'm happy to be here. This afternoon, I get to share the rest of Thanksgiving with my ex-in-laws."

Merv leaned toward Luke. "That sounds like as much fun as riding a horse on a burr-crusted blanket!" His voice was loud enough for everyone to hear.

Donna laughed. Then, just like cascading dominoes, laughter slid around the table.

Nan was still chuckling as she walked toward Luke and Dad on her way to the kitchen. She paused beside them. "It's good to see you smile." She nodded at Dad.

"Nice to have something to smile about."

Nan's lips tipped down into a scowl and the green of her eyes disappeared into narrowed slits. She stared at Dad, quickly drew in a deep breath, and set her hand on Luke's shoulder. "You have a son. He's something to smile about." She spun around and walked into the kitchen.

———

Nan and two of the people who worked for her brought out bowls and plates brimming over with hot food. After setting the turkey in the middle of the table, Nan waited for everyone to quiet down so her father could ask a blessing. His prayer included gratitude for the opportunity to be together with friends and family. Luke added a hearty amen.

When Luke started on his second piece of pumpkin pie, Nan stood up. She thanked everyone for helping her celebrate not only Thanksgiving but also the beginning of the Christmas season.

"As is our custom, I have papers and pencils for those of you who would like to write down your first Wonder for the year." Nan pulled a box of pencils and a stack of small, white papers from a serving cart and set them on the table. "I'll be right back with my Christmas Wonders."

Donna looked at her watch. "Thanks, Nan." She stood, wrote on one of the slips of paper, and handed it to Merv. "That burr-crusted blanket is calling my name. Will you put this in Nan's Christmas Wonders for me?" She waved on her way out.

"Finish your pie and come home," Dad said to Luke and then nodded at Merv. Dad cupped his hands around his mouth, called a thank you to Nan, and left the diner.

While Luke waited for his food to settle so he could eat his last few bites, he observed the remaining guests. Nobody else seemed in a hurry to leave. They visited, filled their dessert plate with more pie, or wrote on the slips of paper.

"Here's my Christmas Wonders," Nan said returning to the room. She held a wrapped package with a small slit in the top.

Luke set his fork on the plate, whipped cream still smooth along the tines. He rubbed his hand up and down his arm, tracing the tiny prickles which had started there but then flowed along his spine. His eyes grew wide and his body stilled as he stared at Christmas Wonders. The commotion in the room seemed out of place.

Merv swapped a story with the man at the end of the table.

They laughed.

Luke looked toward Nan. She picked up the turkey plate and held it out to her parents. Her father took a small piece and popped it in his mouth.

Luke sat back in his chair, relaxing his shoulders. Eyes focused on Christmas Wonders, he lifted a dollop of whipped cream to his mouth savoring its smooth sweetness before it melted away. Then he took a bite of the pie.

Many of the guests had left the room before Merv looked at Luke and pushed his chair back. "How 'bout going with me to thank Nan?"

As they walked side by side, Luke's eyes darted to Christmas Wonders like a hummingbird seeking nectar from a red trumpet vine.

Merv dropped his papers into the slit on top of Christmas Wonders. "I hope you'll join us in our tradition."

Luke reached out and brushed his hand on the side of Christmas Wonders and then pressed his finger along the small slit. Nan touched his back.

"Thanks for Thanksgiving," he said looking up into her face. "That was the best pumpkin pie in the world."

"You're very welcome." She chuckled and warmth glowed in her eyes as she looked at Luke with his hand still on Christmas Wonders. "Thanksgiving used to be my favorite holiday. But now, with Christmas Wonders—well, it's a toss-up."

CHAPTER FOUR

The following morning, Luke washed the breakfast dishes and swept the floor after Dad went to the cobbler shop. At times like this, restlessness crept into his soul. He was bored. Being the only kid who lived in town wasn't the same as being the only kid on the ranch. There, Grandpa usually had a project waiting for him, or he could spend time with Sassy, his gentle mare. He glanced out the small window over the kitchen sink. Everything was dark; gray sky, blacktop covered parking lot, drab cars. Luke turned away. He checked in with Dad and then wandered out the cobbler shop door. Carma often had small jobs around the bookstore, so Luke started down the sidewalk.

"Hi, Luke. Help yourself to the hot chocolate," Carma greeted him as she always did.

Luke filled a cup with the hot, bubbly drink and set it on the children's reading table. Chocolate steam warmed the air. He leaned over the mug, closed his eyes, and breathed in the sweet aroma, savoring it like a cherished memory.

His simple response was the same each time he found his way to the bookstore. The first time Carma invited him in for a cup of hot chocolate, he refused because he didn't have money to pay for it.

"There's no charge." She shook her head, then tilted it as she gazed at him. "Hmm. It's been a while since someone said anything about paying."

He turned away from her open invitation.

"Hey," she called before he left the shop, "I could use some help stocking shelves. How about a trade?"

"Really?" Luke hesitated for only a moment before following her to the hot chocolate machine.

Carma's bookstore had become one of Luke's favorite places. He was always welcome, but perhaps more important—needed.

As soon as Luke drank down the last drop of the sweet chocolate, he went to Carma's side, awaiting her instruction.

She handed him a box of Christmas lights. "Will you straighten those cords and make sure each bulb works?"

Between customers, Carma pulled Christmas wreathes, ribbons, and brightly colored ornaments from a larger box. "There it is," she said aloud, drawing Luke's attention away from his task. She retrieved a wrapped package from the box and set it next to the cash register.

Luke gulped, eyes wide. He looked at his arms, expecting a replay of the sensations from the previous day, but when nothing happened he stepped toward Christmas Wonders.

"That looks like Nan's."

Carma nodded. "It is like Nan's. Lina gave one to each shop owner on this street. Of course, she gave it to my parents. I was away at college, but I always felt it belonged to me too."

He picked it up and jiggled it softly. His eyes narrowed. "It feels empty."

"Uh huh." She looked toward the front door at a group of teenagers huddled by the display widow.

Luke turned it over. It had different dimensions than Nan's, but the paper—printed with musical notes, harps, and angels in long flowing gowns—was the same. He studied it, biting at his bottom lip. "This paper looks so . . . so . . ." He dropped his eye, searching for the memory that hovered just beyond his grasp. Then, shaking his head he shrugged. "What's it for?" he asked, returning it to the small shelf.

"Our Christmas Wonders," Carma said as though that explanation was enough to give him understanding.

"Wonders? I don't—"

"Christmas Wonders . . ." She stopped searching

through the box and glanced once again at the now empty store front. Motioning for Luke to follow her, she walked across the room, pulled out two chairs, and invited him to sit. "Since you live here now, you need to know about Lina and Christmas Wonders. It's a very important part of our town." She leaned forward and waited until their eyes met. "I think I told you Lina lived in the apartment where you live now."

Luke nodded. He recognized the girl's name. Carma mentioned her the first time they met after exclaiming over his piercing blue eyes with the dark green ring. She had stared at him for an unusual amount of time, laughed with a high-pitched twitter, and then told him he had the same color of eyes as her former neighbor.

"Lina and her mother only lived there a couple of years," Carma continued, "but she touched all of our lives. From what I understand, she wasn't well. The Christmas before they left, Lina gave every shop owner a gift just like that one." Carma nodded toward the shelf by the cash register. "'It's for your Christmas Wonders,' she said, and people around here took it to heart. Now it represents the essence of the holidays."

Luke listened attentively. Most nine-year-old boys would have asked several questions. Luke asked just one. "But what is a Christmas Wonder?"

"Ah, that's the question, isn't it? Christmas Wonders are different for each person, so I don't know what your Wonders are. A Christmas Wonder is something you see, hear, smell, touch, or feel that reminds you of Christmas."

Luke turned away.

"It's very simple." Carma put her hand on his arm. "Just think about a Christmas celebration. Write a few words about it on the paper and drop it in the box."

"How do you celebrate Christmas?"

"You don't . . ." She put her hand to her mouth, the creases along her forehead tightening. "Hmm." Tapping her foot on the floor, she began to hum.

Luke watched her, listening, and his eyes softened at the sound.

She stopped humming. "Do you recognize that?"

He nodded.

"How about singing it with me?" She didn't wait for him to agree before starting "Silent Night."

Luke joined her on the second word. He sang with gusto; he seldom had the chance to share music with someone.

Carma quit singing at the end of the first phrase. Luke continued a few notes then trailed to a stop.

"I'm sorry. I was listening to the words you were singing." Carma laughed softly. "I haven't heard those words in years. Will you sing it for me?"

Luke tipped his head and shoved his hands in his pockets.

Carma put her finger under his chin. "Please," she said, encouraging him to meet her eyes.

Hesitant at first, his voice was so quiet the words barely

escaped his mouth; the familiar tune was lost in the noise of the old building.

"Silent night, peaceful night. All is calm, all is right." His volume increased and though he looked toward Carma, his moist eyes seemed to focus beyond her. "When a mother is holding her child. You're my treasure, so tender and mild." His voice grew soft and gentle like a lullaby. "Sleep, while stars shine on high. Sleep, 'til morning is nigh."

Carma's face beamed. She drew in a deep breath and squeezed it slowly between tight lips. "Thanks, Luke. You've just given me a Christmas Wonder."

Luke leaned forward, his face turned up, eyes searching. "Why?"

"Music always touches my heart, and those words are a lullaby I haven't heard for a long, long time." She paused and looked away as though seeking something beyond the time and place to which they were bound. Then she smiled. Warmth shimmered in her eyes. "Where did you learn it?"

Luke shrugged. It must have been his mother, but the memory wasn't clear in his mind. He was perplexed at the possibility that memories of her were slipping away when he needed each one to last his whole life. He pointed to Lina's gift, putting the question behind him by asking one of his own. "Why is it empty?"

Carma stood and walked over to the large box she had been sorting. "Every year, after the holidays, I put the Christmas Wonders in a scrapbook. Here," she said, pulling out a red binder, "why don't you take a look? Maybe it'll help you understand."

Luke sat in one of the overstuffed chairs in the corner and opened the book to the first page. White slips of paper with written notes lined up in rows.

Smell of melting chocolate in Mom's kitchen
Baby Jesus
Wreath on Grandma's door
Singing carols around the piano
Snowflakes
Holding hands with gloves on
Hiding gifts with Dad
Horse-drawn sleigh ride

After turning the page, he paused. Those things sounded nice, but they didn't mean anything to him. He scanned the slips of writing, skipping part of the hand printed notes until he reached the middle of the book. A note written in red crayon caught his eye—*Dad reading the Bible on Christmas Eve.*

Looking up from the book, he gazed out the window. Dark clouds hung low above the city, threatening a storm, much like a day last spring when he finished his chores and ran into the house to get away from the late mountain snow. While waiting for Dad and Grandpa to come in for the evening, he pulled a book off the shelf. A small book nestled in front of it. Settling himself in the wooden rocker, he started the first page of the small book. He didn't even read to the bottom of the first column when he lost interest in the list of difficult names. While returning the book to its spot, Grandpa stepped through the door of the cabin.

Seeing the book in Luke's hand, he stopped and peered into Luke's eyes. "You found your mother's Bible." Grandpa took the book from Luke and flipped through the pages. "Look here," he said, pointing to the top of a page.

"Luke?" he read and then muttered, "It's . . . my name."

"I think this is where your mother got your name." Grandpa turned the page, still holding it so Luke could see the writing. "She used to read the Bible to us after dinner." A smile flickered across his face before he closed his eyes and shook his head as though trying to push away an almost forgotten memory. When he looked back at Luke, he started to speak, but had to stop and clear his throat. He rocked the book gently with one hand. "I haven't seen this book since . . . well, since right after she died." His voice quivered. "Your dad didn't want anything around that reminded him of her or of . . . of God."

"What's it about?" Luke leaned closer so he could see the words.

"Let's get dinner ready. If your dad still isn't done with his chores, I'll read you her favorite part. It's right here in the book of Luke." Grandpa left the book open on the counter while they prepared dinner. After putting the food in the oven, they sat together on the floor by the fire and Grandpa read without even looking at the words. "And it came to pass in those days, that there went out a decree from Caesar Augustus . . ."

Firelight cast flickering shadows around the room and lit Grandpa's face, erasing the look of weariness. Penetrating warmth enveloped Luke as Grandpa's deep voice and soothing lilt danced along the unfamiliar words. He leaned against Grandpa's shoulder, tired enough to nod off, but determined to hear the story his mother loved. Joseph, Mary, the baby Jesus. Names he knew from other books in his mother's collection.

"And suddenly there was with the angel a multitude of the heavenly host . . ." Grandpa's voice softened to a whisper, "and on earth peace, good will—"

The mountain storm blew a chill into the room when Dad opened the cabin door. Without a word, Grandpa closed the book and pushed it back into the hidden cubby.

The next time Luke was alone in the house, he retrieved the Bible and found the verse where Grandpa stopped reading. Although he was able to read a few verses on his own, it wasn't the same. The words were difficult to sound out, and he couldn't understand the language. What flowed smoothly in Grandpa's voice seemed like a foreign language when reading it alone. Yet, he felt compelled to seek it out again; a name is such a personal connection. However, the second time he reached inside the hidden cubby, the book was gone. Pulling out each book on the shelf, he searched for the Bible until he was sure it was no longer there. He planned to ask Grandpa about it, but after that, due to spring calving and getting the cattle herd to the range, he forgot about his mother's hidden Bible—until now.

A sick feeling jumped in the pit of his stomach. He hadn't seen it during their move. Maybe it was with the other books. Before they drove away from the ranch, Dad gave a sack of his mother's books to one of the cowboys. Luke wanted to jump out of the pickup and retrieve her books; instead, he pulled the door shut. He had no say in the matter.

Luke looked back at the list of Wonders. As he turned the page, he saw another red crayon note—*Nan's Thanksgiving dinner.*

He read it again—something familiar. But what made Nan's Thanksgiving dinner a Christmas Wonder? The invitation itself had been important to him. But a Wonder? And then there was the food—the pumpkin pie. His mouth watered. And the people. What was it Merv thanked Nan for? Something about getting a crowd together. Luke shrugged, unable to connect the two.

He closed the book and carried it to the shelf by the cash register. Carma was ringing up a sale. She put the customer's book in a bag, counted his change, and then looked up into his eyes. They smiled at each other. "Have a wonder-filled Christmas," she said. Her voice sounded like music.

"Thank you. I'm sure I will." The man picked up a small piece of paper, wrote on it, and dropped it into the opening on the top of Christmas Wonders.

Another customer came through the door before Luke could talk to Carma. With a wave of his hand, he told her he was leaving.

"Luke," she called to him as she walked toward the customer. "When you think of a Christmas Wonder, I'd love you to put it with mine."

CHAPTER FIVE

Luke zipped up his light jacket as a north wind blew down the narrow road, catching him in the clutches of an approaching storm. He wove through the semi-crowded walks. A change was taking place in the city. The drabness that accompanied the end of autumn's generous color was transitioning into a man-made display. Workers hung lights from lampposts and shop owners trimmed the windows of their stores. He had never seen anything like it.

Instead of heading to his apartment, he slowly made his way past Nan's Diner to get a smell of the morning baking. He paused at the corner, checked out the scenery to the right and the left, and then headed across the street. People milled on the lawn of the town square. He wandered closer to see what they were doing.

"Hey, Luke," someone in the group called.

He searched the crowd. Merv waved. Luke walked toward him.

"Do you want to help us?" Merv asked, setting down a large, tarp-covered bundle. Not waiting for an answer, he put his hand on Luke's shoulder and guided him to the back of a truck. "Can you carry this?" He placed a small bundle in Luke's arms. "It's for the . . ." He stopped, looked into Luke's eyes, and smiled. "It's good to have your help; it reminds me of when Lina lived here. It must have been the Christmas before she left. You know, she loved the nativity. I think she's the one who taught us to make it the center of our Christmas celebration."

Luke tilted his head, his eyebrows knit together as he listened to Merv reminisce. Then, following his lead, Luke carried the small bundle to the podium. The two of them retrieved each item from the truck until it was unloaded.

"We're ready," Merv called through cupped hands as he stepped up the stairs to the platform. "Everybody gather 'round."

The people who had been decorating stopped their work and "gathered 'round." They laughed and greeted one another with a handshake or a welcoming hug, until Merv began uncovering a long bundle. Then, as if someone had called them to attention, the group quieted down and turned to watch.

After removing the tarp, Merv turned the statuette toward the crowd. The entire group smiled and nodded.

Merv stepped over to the next one. Each time he uncovered a statuette and set it upright on the podium, the group smiled and nodded.

When Merv picked up the last bundle, a unified silence settled on the group. Merv held it as a mother cradles her baby, his face alight with a tender smile. The group waited, as though willing him time to perform a precious ritual.

Before unwrapping it, Merv turned and looked at the crowd until his eyes rested on Luke. With a tilt of his head he said, "Luke, come on up here."

Luke stepped back, his eyes round, mouth agape. He had never been in front of so many people. The group turned to him—smiling, nodding, waiting. His heart pounded. Should he run to Merv or away from the crowd? He glanced at the bundle. Still tightly wrapped to protect . . . what? He pushed his shoulders back and jumped onto the podium.

Merv extended the bundle toward him. "Here, you uncover it."

Gently, Luke removed the tarp. He stared at the tiny statuette. "Baby Jesus," he whispered, tracing the baby's cheek with his finger.

The group began singing. Merv waited until Luke pulled his hand away from the Christ Child's face. Then he set the small statuette inside of what looked like a little box.

Luke followed Merv from the podium. They stood in the midst of the group until the song about a baby, a manger, and the Lord Jesus trailed to a close. There was still an expression of confusion on Luke's face, though it softened when he looked at the Christ Child. Everyone around him seemed united, linked together in a common purpose and understanding. As the crowd dispersed, many called out, "Have a wonder-filled Christmas."

Merv slipped his arm around Luke's shoulders. "Thanks for helping with the baby Jesus."

Luke glanced at Merv's hand on his shoulder and then turned his head so he could see his face. Although he recognized each one of the statuettes from the story Grandpa read, there was something he couldn't understand.

"Umm . . . Why . . . ?" He hesitated, and dropped his head.

"Yes?" Merv bent over, his eyes on Luke's face.

Luke leaned close to Merv's ear and whispered, "Why is the baby in a box?"

"A box?" He shook his head. "Oh," he chuckled quietly. "That's a manger. Baby Jesus was born in a stable. They used a manger for a . . ." Merv stopped, his gaze on the baby lying in his accustomed place. "Someone else asked me that." He put his finger to his mouth before looking back at Luke. "Sorry. Your question—it's déjà vu. The manger was used like a cradle for the Christ Child."

———————

While helping Merv return the tarps to the pickup, snow began falling. Half-dollar sized flakes melted and seeped through Luke's light jacket. He shivered and turned toward home to find his winter clothes.

Dad barely looked up from his worktable when Luke walked through the door of the cobbler shop. They didn't have the custom of greeting one another, so Luke didn't speak as he hurried across the worn tiles to the adjoining apartment. He walked from box to box, looking for some sort of identification to guide him. Finally, he started with a large box, light enough for him to move from the dark corner to the middle of the room.

He pulled the cardboard flaps open. His gloves were on top. Somewhere inside he was sure to find a coat and boots. However, he didn't recognize the tiny snow pants and coats packed under the gloves. He held them up and studied each one. They must have been his. Now they were of no use to anyone. He set them on a chair and turned his attention back to the box.

When he was halfway through the pile of winter clothing, he saw a light blue, furry, one-piece snow suit. It had feet and a hood—just the thing to keep an infant warm. Even though it wasn't what he was looking for, he picked it up and held it against his face, relishing the soft material and the scent—his mother. He closed his eyes, lost in the moment of wanting her, feeling her there—almost.

He didn't even notice the tears that trickled from his eyes and dropped upon the tiny blue suit, or the minutes that slipped by as he held it close and felt—he couldn't put a word to that feeling. Blurred memories of his toddler years flitted through his mind, giving him a glimpse of what it was like then, yet remaining too elusive to hold onto.

It was not until he heard Dad open the door to their apartment that he set the blue suit on the chair and turned his mind back to the present. He wiped at his eyes and twisted toward the wall so Dad wouldn't see his face.

Looking back into the box, he saw a tiny red scarf. He pushed it aside, uncovering a figurine. It seemed strange to find something like that among old winter clothes until he realized it was a perfect place to pack something fragile. The soft clothing had protected it.

His breath slipped out in an amazed acknowledgement as he lifted it from the box. Perhaps, if he had seen it some other time, he wouldn't have understood the small, porcelain figurine. But, having just taken part in the unveiling of a nativity, he knew immediately what it was—mother Mary and the baby Jesus. Lifelike, colored features shone on the face of the young woman, and she held the baby Jesus in her arms: close, protecting, lovingly hugged against her body.

Luke stared at the figurine. The baby's eyes were closed in slumber. But it was Mary who grabbed his attention. Her face shone with—he couldn't find the right word, but he knew it—something tender, intangible—something he had just felt.

"What are you doing?" Dad's harsh voice caught him by surprise.

Luke jumped, his hands tightened around Mary and the baby. "Loo . . . looking for a coat," he stammered, setting the figurine on the table.

Dad walked past him to the kitchen sink. He filled a glass with water, gulped it down, and pulled out a day-old sandwich from the refrigerator. Turning toward the table, he pointed to the figurine. "What's that?"

"Something for Christmas."

"We don't do Christmas." Dad moved the pile of old, winter clothing from the chair to the table, almost knocking off the figurine.

Luke grabbed it. Holding it like Merv had held the statuette of Jesus at the town square, he searched for a safe place to set it. Dad reached out and took it.

"This was Evangel—your mother's. I thought she . . ." His voice faded to a whisper. He turned the figurine around in his hands, gazing at it from every angle. Shaking his head, he set it on the table in front of him and exhaled a ragged breath

"Your mother loved this." He cleared his throat, and then, as though side-stepping a rattler, he shifted to the other side of the table. "She said it was the way it was supposed to be." The tenderness in his voice changed to scorn. "Whatever that means."

Although Luke continued his search for a coat and boots until he reached the bottom of the box, he wasn't disappointed not to find them. His search gave him something to do until Dad finished his lunch and returned to the shop.

As soon as Dad left, Luke stuffed the winter clothes back in the box and picked up the figurine. This was his mother's. This was something she loved. Dad's comment about it being the way it was supposed to be made perfect sense to Luke.

Tenderly, he set the figurine on the small shelf by the kitchen window, pulled on his jacket, and ran through the shop to the front door. Something was pushing him, a feeling of excitement, of belonging somehow to something he didn't comprehend—until now.

He ran down the sidewalk and rushed into the bookstore. Carma waved at him from the back of the room. Returning her wave, he continued on his way to the cash register. He picked up one of the papers and a pencil. In his best penmanship, he wrote five words and dropped the paper through the top of Christmas Wonders.

CHAPTER SIX

L uke hurried through the fog, past the shops and the town square with barely a glance on his way to school. It wasn't until he reached the school block that he slowed his pace. He hadn't walked this way since the day before Thanksgiving, and the transformation that took place in those few days made him stare in amazement. It looked like a Christmas festival. Each home sported decorations that filled the empty spaces on the winter-brown lawns, and the lights that still glowed broke through the fog as a lantern in the night.

Mesmerized by his surroundings, he didn't even hear the noise of the schoolyard until he was at the fence that ran along the grounds. For a moment, he felt disappointed to see the decorations end, but, as he approached the front walk, he saw something that made him stop. Two huge pine trees on either side of the sidewalk that led to the school were draped in tiny white lights, like ethereal candles. Shining through the fog, the top lights faded into the dark, giving one the impression that there was no treetop, no end to the heavenly glow.

When the first bell rang, he ran up the stairs and opened the heavy, wooden door. A large, square, brick display with two legs coming out the middle sat just inside. He stopped in front of it, wondering what it could possibly be until two older boys walked by.

"Haha," one of them said, pointing at the legs. "Santa got caught."

Down the hall, tiny cottages and shops, white with snow, sparkled under colored lights in the glass showcase. Large posters of Christmas candy, toys, and presents covered the walls.

It wasn't until he slipped into his seat that he had time to look around his classroom. Everything looked different there as well. All the fall pictures and displays were gone. White papers, covered with writing and mounted on red and green construction paper, hung in their place. He stared at the one closest to him, but couldn't make out the small printing.

"Welcome back," Mrs. Layne said after the second bell rang. "I hope you enjoyed your break." She glanced around the room and smiled. "Now, we can prepare for the Christmas season. I like to decorate with Christmas letters." She pointed with both hands along the walls. "Read them so you can see how to compose your own. Letters are written for many . . ."

Luke tried to pay attention as Mrs. Layne explained the purpose and format of letters, but he was more interested in actually reading them than in hearing about them. When she finished teaching the proper way to write a letter, she gave an assignment to write one.

"Envelopes," she said, "are in the corner of the writing table for those who want to mail a letter. Or, if you'd prefer, I'll mount your letter on construction paper and take it to one of our local stores. Shop owners like to display them for the season.

"The letters on the walls were written by students. These three letters," she said, pointing to a small bulletin board at the front of the room, "were written to me. I like to share them because they're very special Christmas letters. Any questions?"

Tami raised her hand. "Who do we write to?" She asked Luke's question.

"You may write to anyone you'd like. For example, write to grandparents, aunts, uncles, cousins, friends, or, of course, Santa." She pointed to the letters on the wall by Luke's desk.

Her answer didn't help Luke. He didn't have a grandparent, aunt, uncle, cousin, or friend to write. And Santa? Well, he'd read stories about Santa, but he didn't have anything to say to him.

After turning in his science assignment, Luke strolled past the letters by his desk. Each was addressed "Dear Santa." Most of them were lists of requests; he gave them only a cursory glance. A very short letter with chicken scratch writing caught his attention. He couldn't identify most of the words. However, at the bottom, after a P.S., the words were clear. *Have a wonder-filled Christmas. Platt.*

Luke looked back to the top of the letter and slowly made out part of the writing. Platt didn't ask for anything. His letter was simply a thank-you note.

Mrs. Layne excused the class a little early for recess so they could have time to look at the letters before going outside. Luke walked to the front of the room. Stopping by the bulletin board, he saw that each of his teacher's "special letters" was addressed "Dear Tia." The first one was from Grandma, the second was from Mom, and the third one—he barely got to it when Grace came up beside him.

"That one's from Lina, the girl who started Christmas Wonders," she said.

"How do you know?"

"My mom told me. She and Tia—I mean, Mrs. Layne—and Lina were friends." Grace pointed to the bottom of the letter. "See what she wrote."

Luke looked at the P.S. *You are a Christmas Wonder.*

———

Mrs. Layne handed everyone a piece of white stationary. After reading many of the letters, Luke was confident about the format. And since he had decided whom to write, he began at once. When he finished the letter, he went to the writing desk, picked up an envelope, and wrote a name on the front.

Just before the bell rang, Mrs. Layne gave her final instructions. "Please put your letter in the writing file. If you have an envelope, clip it to the letter and bring the address tomorrow."

Luke leaned back in his chair, his eyes narrowed. He hadn't heard Mrs. Layne mention an address. Not knowing what to do, he waited until all the students left the room before plodding up to her desk.

"Yes, Luke?"

"I don't know her address."

"That's all right. Get it from your dad tonight."

Luke shook his head. "He doesn't know her."

"He doesn't know her?" Mrs. Layne took the envelope from his outstretched hand, her eyes scanned over the name. "You have to have a last name." She set the envelope in front of him.

"What is her last name?"

"Whose?" Mrs. Layne tilted her head, her forehead scrunched into wrinkles.

"Lina."

"Lina?" Mrs. Layne stopped and took a deep breath. "Luke, I can't help you if you don't know her last name."

Luke pointed to the letter behind her desk. "She's *your* friend."

Mrs. Layne turned around, her eyes following his finger. "You wrote a letter to Lina?" She glanced at the envelope then back at Luke's face.

He nodded.

"How . . . how nice," she stammered with a tight laugh. "I'm sure she'd be delighted, but I don't have her address. I haven't heard from her since we were girls."

"Oh . . . um . . ." He looked at the letter and shrugged his shoulders.

"Hmm. Maybe I can find the address," Mrs. Layne said to herself as much as to Luke. "Leave your letter and envelope here. I'll see if I can find out where—" She stopped and nodded her head. "Thanks, Luke. I'd love to get in touch with Lina."

As Luke turned and left, Mrs. Layne glanced at the envelope, letting her mind slip back through time, purposely grasping each memory of Lina. Thoughts of that gentle, loving friend filled her with a sweet remembrance that turned her tentative possibility of finding Lina into a firm commitment. Before Lina moved away, they promised to stay in touch. After exchanging letters for a year, Mrs. Layne didn't know what to do when her letter to Lina was returned marked "undeliverable." With no way to communicate, their friendship faded away.

Setting the envelope down, she picked up Luke's letter and glanced over it. He used the correct format.

Dear Lina,

I live in the apartment you lived in. My dad fixes shoes. I used to live on a ranch. I miss home, but I like the people here.

Mrs. Layne is my teacher. She is very nice. Grace said she is your friend.

Thank you for Christmas Wonders. It makes people smile.

I hope you have a very nice Christmas. I want one, too.

From,
Luke

P.S. I found a Christmas Wonder.

She looked out the window, amused but not surprised by the unusual letter. From the first day Luke came into her classroom, he had done things outside the norm for children his age. Perusing the letter again, she smiled. It would probably make Lina smile, she thought, hoping to share it with her friend. She folded the letter and put it in the envelope.

After mounting five of her students' letters on green and red paper, she put them in a manila folder and carried them to the car. She could take care of two errands at once—pick up her book order and drop off the letters for Carma to display.

CHAPTER SEVEN

Mrs. Layne walked into the bookstore and held up the manila folder so Carma could see it before setting it on the counter. "I've got you a present."

"Great, you brought me letters. I can't wait to read them," Carma said. Then she turned to riffle through her files and pulled out the delivery confirmation on Mrs. Layne's order. "Come in and look around while I get your books."

Mrs. Layne laughed. "Wow, you're good. You know I'll find more books I can't live without."

"*That* would be the point," Carma bantered on her way into the storage room.

"How is the Christmas Wonders Program coming?" Mrs. Layne asked after paying for her order.

"Pretty good." Carma picked up the manila folder, pulled out the mounted letters, and glanced through them. "Two people volunteered to share their Christmas Wonder, and I know of one other person I want to ask, but I'd like a couple of children on the program." She stopped and picked up a blank, white envelope from the middle of the mounted letters. "Is this for me?"

"No, sorry." Mrs. Layne took the envelope. "It was on my desk. I must have picked it up with your letters."

Carma looked up after skimming through the last mounted letter. "Do you know someone who could share a Wonder?"

"Let me think about . . . maybe." She looked down at the envelope in her hand. "I'm not sure if it's a Wonder, but the most unusual thing happened this year. One of my students wrote a letter to Lina. I've had students write Christmas letters for years and this is the first time someone—"

"Your student wrote to Lina . . . hmm. Is that something we could use on the program?"

Mrs. Layne turned the envelope over so the name was on the top and held it out to Carma. "I don't know. You decide."

Carma glanced at the envelope. "This is it?"

Mrs. Layne nodded.

Carma pulled out the single sheet of paper. "Wait a minute." She looked up from the letter and held it toward

Mrs. Layne. "Luke? This has to be Luke Cardston."

"You know him?" Mrs. Layne's forehead wrinkled. Luke had barely moved to town and he wasn't exactly outgoing.

"He lives in the apartment behind the cobbler shop. He comes here quite often. In fact, he helped me put up my Christmas decorations and said the strangest thing. It . . . it really bothered me." She shook her head. "He asked me how you celebrate Christmas, like he didn't have a Christmas memory." She pointed to the letter. "But here—"

"It says he *found* a Wonder." Mrs. Layne had chalked up the P.S. as just one more unusual thing about Luke. But it seemed there was much more to the story. "'Found a Wonder,'" she repeated to herself. "What does that mean?"

Carma put a finger to her mouth, her eyes narrowed. "He ran in here the other day and went right over to Christmas Wonders. I had a customer, so I didn't talk to him, but he seemed different—excited actually. He was only here a minute—" She glanced at the shelf by the cash register. "Hey, maybe he put in a Wonder."

"Hmm . . . I've never heard anyone say they *found* a Wonder. It'd be interesting to know what he was talking about." Mrs. Layne's eyebrows rose. "Wouldn't it?"

"We can find out."

Mrs. Layne shrugged. "I don't see a problem; it's not private."

Carma took the top off Christmas Wonders.

Since the holiday season had just begun, there were

only a few Wonders in the box. Mrs. Layne reached for one in a child's hand and held it next to Luke's letter. She nodded to Carma.

"*The mother holding her baby*," Carma said Luke's Wonder aloud. "What does that mean?"

Mrs. Layne glanced up from the note just as someone walked through the front door. She cleared her throat and poked Carma with her elbow. Carma followed Mrs. Layne's gaze and then blurted a sharp laugh. Had they been caught snooping?

"Luke . . ." Mrs. Layne's voice cracked. She and Carma started to talk at the same time as though they were carrying on a routine conversation that didn't include him. They stopped talking, in unison, looked at each other, and chuckled.

Luke hadn't said a word since entering the store. Standing just inside the door, he stuck his hands in the pockets of his pants and stared at the women. It wasn't until Mrs. Layne motioned for him to come in and join them that he walked forward.

Carma slid the Wonders back in the box, slipped the top on, and pushed Christmas Wonders into its appointed spot. "Hey, I just had an idea." She raised her eyebrows at Mrs. Layne and then focused on Luke. "You've been learning about some of our traditions, right? On Christmas morning, we have a program so people can share a Wonder. Your teacher showed me the letter you wrote Lina. I'd like to add it to the program. How about reading it? And then you can tell everyone why you wanted to write to . . ."

Luke's eyes flew open. Without turning around, he inched toward the door.

"Luke." Mrs. Layne held out a hand and walked toward him. "You don't have to do it." Her voice was soothing, as though quieting a startled horse.

"Of course you don't." Carma laughed softly and then pulled in a deep breath. "I just think it's nice you wanted to thank Lina."

Although he hadn't run away, his shoulders cowered and his eyes dropped to the floor. Mrs. Layne put her hand on Luke's arm. "We've had students share a Wonder almost every year. We're just looking for ideas. You don't have to take part, but maybe you can help us think of someone we could ask to share a Wonder." She waited, not really expecting an answer.

With the fear edging from his face, he lifted his eyes to Mrs. Layne's. An excited awareness seemed to light up his whole being. He blurted out one word, "Lina."

Mrs. Layne flipped around. Her eyes met Carma's. Like a flowing electrical current, Luke's idea buzzed through the air, uniting them. It was perfect. Why hadn't they thought of it before? Lina started their tradition. She deserved to see what her Christmas Wonders had done for the people in their city.

Before entering the bookstore, Mrs. Layne was

determined to find Lina, not only so she could send her Luke's letter, but also to reconnect with her friend. Now, with the hope of inviting Lina as the guest of honor, her resolve strengthened.

Carma handed Mrs. Layne a notepad and pen. The women brainstormed possible avenues for their search.

"I'll get a hold of Lina's old friends," Mrs. Layne said, writing on her paper.

"Good idea." Carma's chin dipped. "Many of the shop owners knew Lina and her mother. I'll pay them a visit; maybe someone has kept in touch."

Mrs. Layne looked up from her paper. "Oh, yes and—"

"Do you think," Luke said, stepping closer to the women, "I can help?"

CHAPTER EIGHT

Carma and Luke decided to begin their search by visiting Merv. Lina's mother had worked for him. They planned an after school visit the following day while Carma's assistant could look after the bookstore.

Carma pushed the door to Merv's shoe store open and motioned for Luke to go in before her. They waited until Merv counted back the change to his only customer.

"Hi, Merv. We're on a mission to get information about Lina," Carma said. "Luke suggested we invite her for our Christmas program."

"It would be great to see her again."

"I thought you'd like the idea." Carma tipped her head toward Luke. "Our young friend here found a Christmas Wonder."

Merv eyed Luke with an inquisitive stare. When Luke didn't say anything, he looked back at Carma. "Oh?"

Carma shrugged.

"Well, Luke, it looks like you have everybody's curiosity up. Will you tell us what you found?" Merv asked.

"It was my mother's," Luke said.

"What was?"

"The nativity." Luke stopped as though that was explanation enough. When neither Merv nor Carma picked up the conversation, he added in a whisper. "Mary was *holding* the baby Jesus."

"Ahhhh." Merv shook one finger. "He wasn't in a box."

Carma laughed. "What?"

"Luke helped with the nativity and asked why baby Jesus was in a box." Merv paused, his eyes stared past them. Then he blurted out a short laugh. "You know, I think Lina asked me that same question. She would have loved your mother's nativity."

He put his hand on Luke's shoulder. "I bet you'll remember your first Wonder 'cause I remember mine."

"Really?" Carma's voice sounded incredulous. "It's been twenty years."

Merv's eyes glazed with memories. "I don't know if you knew my wife, Mamie?"

"Just a little."

"She was an amazing woman. And Lina was . . . how can I put it? Lina was her joy during those last years of life."

Merv tapped his mouth with his fingers, and then shared his memory.

When Lina moved into the apartment with her mother, Mamie was in a wheelchair due to multiple sclerosis. Merv brought her to work with him each day; they depended on each other. Since Lina lived next door and her mother worked at the shoe store, Lina often dropped in to visit. She and Mamie formed an instant bond, both understanding physical weakness and limitations. They also shared a great love for literature, and discovered if they read a story aloud, it merged into near reality, much like seeing it played out on a stage. It was a delight they both needed and loved.

When Lina had difficulty breathing, Mamie read. On those days when Mamie was struggling, Lina read. They went through dozens of books together, but more importantly, they shared a depth of feelings that nourished their souls.

"After Lina gave us Christmas Wonders, Mamie set it by the cash register and encouraged everyone who came in to use it." Merv chuckled. "I think she nearly filled it herself."

"That sounds like my parents. It was such a special part of their celebration," Carma said. "Did you ever hear someone say Christmas Wonders helped save this street?"

"Save the street?" Luke looked at Carma, eyes clouded with confusion.

Merv nodded. "Not the street exactly, but it certainly

helped to keep our little area of town intact."

"Why?" Luke asked.

"It was a rough time. Most of the shops had barely enough business to stay open."

"Hmm. I guess I didn't realize that." Carma shook her head. "Of course, I was away at college so I had other things on my mind."

Merv laughed. "I think your folks were doing all right at the bookstore, but several stores closed right after—"

"Oh, yes—there was a little grocery store and a garden shop and . . ." Carma pursed her lips.

"It felt like a ghost town. Nobody walked down the sidewalk unless they had found a parking spot here. Some days we didn't have a customer."

"What changed?" Carma asked.

"I'm sure the answer is pretty complicated. And it obviously took a combination of factors to turn this area from such a depressed state to what it is today. But, as strange as it may seem, I credit Christmas Wonders with being the catalyst—"

"Huh?" Carma chuckled. "Now, Merv! I'm a fan of Christmas Wonders. But really?"

He held up one hand. "You asked. All I can tell you is what Mamie and I observed." He cleared his throat and plunged on. "The year Lina gave us her gift, Mamie noticed people dropped in our store before going down the road. It was amazing how many Wonders we had that year. We realized the change started when people began to *look* for something positive to put in Christmas Wonders. It felt good to be a part of that tradition."

Carma leaned forward, her index finger rested on her lips. She looked at Luke the way adults do when trying to determine if a child "gets it" before turning back to Merv. "I guess you know what you're saying is amazing."

"Mamie used to say, 'gratitude is the foundation for positive feelings.' In order to take part in Christmas Wonders, a person must not only think about what they're grateful for, but they write it down." He turned to Luke. "I think Lina understood that. Christmas Wonders was her way of bringing gratitude into our lives."

"Gratitude?" Luke toyed with the word, trying to connect it with his Christmas Wonder.

"Hmmm . . . I always thought it was about sharing the Christmas Spirit, but perhaps they are one and the same." Carma sighed. "I'll have to think about that."

Merv looked at Luke. "Sorry, Luke. We got off the subject of your Wonder. Where did you find the nativity?"

"Under some winter clothes."

"Did you write it down and put it in Christmas Wonders?"

Luke nodded. "What was your Wonder?"

Merv's shoulders rose, his chest expanded with a deep breath. He exhaled through his mouth as he reached for his Christmas Wonders. "Mamie died just after Thanksgiving. I was so lonely and dreaded Christmas without her." He removed the top and dumped out hundreds of small paper strips into a shoebox, nearly filling it. Then he reached inside and pulled out an envelope.

"I got this letter from Lina a week or two after Mamie passed away." He held it out so Luke could see it. "She wrote to Mamie about being in the hospital. Nights were difficult when her mother had to leave. One evening as she lay crying in her bed, a little girl who had just been admitted walked over, took her hand, and told her she wasn't alone. Jesus was there for her because he loved her and . . ." Merv squeezed his eyes tight several times.

Luke moved closer to Merv's side, his eyes straining at the letter. Merv held it out and pointed to the bottom of the page.

"Here," he said. "Lina wrote a note to me. Can you read that?"

There was a P.S. next to Merv's finger. Luke read aloud, "Merv, Jesus loves you, too."

"That was my Christmas Wonder." Although Merv's voice softened, there was power in his words. "I felt His love."

Nobody spoke for several moments. Merv touched Luke's shoulder and waited until their eyes met. "Luke, Lina would want you to know Jesus loves *you*."

Luke stared at Merv, his face alight. The room filled with a warm, penetrating tenderness. Heaven's love seemed approachable, close, as though it surrounded them.

Carma drew in a sharp breath. Her eyes pooled with softness.

The alarm on the front door beeped. A customer entered and called out a greeting to Merv. The moment—that wonderful moment of feeling connected with pure love—faded. Merv folded the letter and put it back in the bottom of his Christmas Wonders.

"I'll see if I can find any of the other letters Lina wrote. Perhaps they could help you," Merv said. "Oh, and you ought to talk to Howie. He was good friends with Lina's mother."

━━━━━━━━━━━━━━

Although Luke and Carma left the shoe store together, they went different directions outside. Carma headed to the bookstore. Luke turned toward the town square.

He needed to be alone, to contemplate the amazing feelings he just experienced. Hardly noticing the canopy of Christmas lights, or the display of holiday scenes, he walked toward the nativity. Stopping in front of the platform, he thought about Jesus—not just about His birth, but, more important at that instant, His love.

When he helped Merv unwrap the statuette and looked down into the face of baby Jesus, a wonderful feeling enfolded his being. After reading Lina's letter, he felt the same feeling. It must be true! As his mind finally comprehended what his heart knew, he headed back along the crowded walk, away from the town square. Retracing his steps, he entered the shoe store, took a small, white piece of paper and wrote *Jesus loves ME*.

ays later, Luke finished his hot chocolate and browsed through a new Christmas book as he waited for Carma. She was busy with a customer and Luke was willing to wait until she could leave the store. They had plans that afternoon to continue the quest to find Lina.

After giving her assistant a few instructions, Carma motioned for Luke to meet her at the door. They crossed the street together and entered Howie's Home of Furniture.

Christmas Wonders sat on a polished, cherry wood desk. Several pencils and small, white slips of paper were next to it.

When the sales clerk asked if he could help them, Carma explained they needed to speak with Howie. He motioned to the nearby chairs, inviting them to sit while he went to get his boss.

Carma walked over to a loveseat and plopped down. "Have a seat, Luke. They want people to try out the furniture."

Having never been in a furniture store, Luke gazed around at the couches and chairs that lined the floor but didn't move toward one. When Carma insisted, he carefully scooted into a large, brown recliner. Carma leaned her head back and closed her eyes. Luke sat still for a couple of seconds before bouncing his legs on the stiff leather as he assessed the many possibilities. Taking Carma at her word, he squirmed out of the brown chair and collapsed into the green chair next to it and so on until, by the time Howie came to greet them, he had tried out half the recliners in the row.

"Hello, Carma and . . ."

"Luke," Carma introduced him. "He and his dad live in the apartment adjoining the cobbler shop."

"Oh, yes. Tell me, Luke. Which chair's best?"

"The green one," Luke pointed to the chair near the front of the store.

Howie laughed. "You have great taste." He turned and waved for them to follow. "Come back here."

Carma explained the reason for their visit as they followed Howie through the store and into his office.

There was a large desk, strewn with papers, in the center of the room with two chairs situated in front of it. The desk was the first thing Luke noticed when they walked through the door, but then his eyes were drawn to the shelf of pictures on the side wall. Carma went right to the pictures, and so Luke followed. Next to a large portrait of a woman and girl was a framed pencil drawing of a man and a child. Both were dressed in robes that flowed from their shoulders to their feet. The man's hand rested on the child's shoulder. Their faces turned upward.

"What a nice picture of your family." Carma glanced at Howie. "What's this picture?" She pointed to the pencil drawing.

Howie flipped through a folder of overflowing papers on his desk. "Two shepherds on the night of the Savior's birth," he said without glancing up to see where Carma was pointing.

"Looks like your daughter's an artist."

Howie shook his head as he motioned for Carma and Luke to sit in the chairs that faced the desk. "Lina gave it to me."

"Lina?" Carma glanced back at the picture.

"She drew it for me right before they left. It was a thank-you gift for helping her and her mother. Remarkable, isn't it?"

Carma sat in the chair farthest from the wall and motioned for Luke to take the other chair. "Yes—and perhaps more remarkable, you have it framed on this shelf."

"Oh, that." Howie shrugged. "Well, since you've come about Lina, I might as well tell you the story."

"We'd like to hear it." Carma leaned forward. "I understand you were friends with Lina's mother. What was her name?"

"Her mother's name is Audra Welton. Her father's name was . . . let me see, Benjamin, I think. Audra and Lina moved here right after he died. They'd only been here about six months when Audra and I met at a town social. She was so beau—" He paused and shifted in his seat. "Anyway, we became friends."

Howie explained that as their friendship grew, so did his feelings, even though Audra told him Lina was her life and she wouldn't marry again. Still, the three of them spent a great deal of time together. When Audra told him they were moving, he left their apartment, slamming the door behind him.

A few days later, Lina brought him the picture. He set it on his desk and didn't think about it again until Audra came to tell him goodbye. She picked up the picture and told him he should feel very special. Lina's gift of the shepherds showed how much she cared for him.

"Of course, I asked why." Howie stopped and looked at Luke. "How old are you, Luke?"

"Nine," Luke said quickly, hoping he would finish the story.

"Hmm . . . Lina must have been a little older than you, but still, she was so mature." He put both hands on his desk and glanced back and forth between his guests. "Anyway,

Audra said Lina loved the shepherds because they listened and obeyed."

Carma pushed her back into the chair, her eyebrows furrowed. "So, did you put it there to remember Lina?"

"No!" He snickered. "I wanted to forget Audra. Lina's picture was filed away until some years later, after I met Jean. Oddly enough, she was the one who framed it and put it there."

"Your wife? That's interesting."

"Jean thought it'd help me remember something. We began dating at Christmas time and she loved Christmas Wonders. One day, while helping me with my files, she came upon that picture." He tilted his head toward the wall. "Jean appreciated Lina's respect for the shepherds, but she also understood what they did from an adult's perspective. She told me the shepherds not only listened and obeyed, but they left something *very* important for something *more* important. This store was my life and I was a . . . " He stopped and shook his index finger. "Oh, what do you call it?"

"A workaholic?" Carma said.

Howie nodded. "She framed that picture for our wedding gift."

Carma and Howie laughed.

Luke seldom laughed and, at that moment, he couldn't; not because he didn't understand the hidden meaning behind their words, but more to the point, he knew Lina was right. That knowledge prompted a reverence toward the story and the picture. It was very clear to him—the shepherds understood.

Luke stood and walked over to the picture. He wanted to hold it, to take it into his soul as a part of himself. Aside from the picture of his mother, it was the only picture that had ever touched him with understanding. When he saw the picture of his mother, he knew love. Now, when he looked at the picture of the shepherds and reflected on why Lina drew them, he was drawn to them in empathy.

Picking up the picture, he noticed something written on the back of the frame. He turned it over and read: *What you do now is a reflection of what you would have done then.*

The words seemed to require a comment, a commitment really, and Luke responded without prompting or interpretation. "I would go." The words slipped from his soul.

"What?" Carma glanced at the empty chair before her eyes sprang to where Luke stood.

At the same instant, Howie pushed himself up and walked to Luke's side, a contemplative smile played on his features.

Luke looked at Howie, his face serious, even a bit fearful as he held out the picture. Had he done something wrong by taking it into his hands?

Howie cleared his throat and rested his hand on Luke's shoulder, holding Luke's eyes with his own. A warmth of understanding spread across his face and rained down on

Luke. "I know you would," he said, his voice soft with awe. "*You* would go as commanded." He tipped his jaw in one quick acknowledgement. "Just like Lina."

Carma looked at her watch. "Oh, no!" she cried. "It's late. I've got to get back to my store."

Since Howie had not accepted the picture from his outstretched hands, Luke acted on his longing to imprint Lina's drawing in his mind, and pulled the picture close so he could focus on the man and child. Howie's eyes were intense on Luke's face, but he didn't seem to notice.

"We've got to go, Luke." Carma was at the door.

With outstretched hands, Luke once again offered the picture to Howie. Howie hesitated, hands at his side, a flash of doubt crossed his eyes.

"Luke," Carma insisted.

Before Howie could respond, Luke set the picture carefully back on the shelf.

As they walked to the front of the furniture store, Howie told Carma he would ask his wife if she kept any of Audra's letters. "It's been a long time, but—"

"That would be great." Carma opened the door and waited until Luke walked out. She followed him to the sidewalk.

━━━━━━━━━━

Howie stood in front of the big picture window, jingling the change in his pocket. Over the years, he had seen many reactions to Lina's drawing. Most people either dismissed it as insignificant or found it a novel art piece for his office display. Some had been interested in the artist. Only a few people turned it over and read the statement on the back. But this was the first time someone had actually understood the significance of the picture and the words. Perhaps that was the reason he felt the urge to give Lina's gift to Luke, but he had hesitated and the moment was lost in Carma's insistence.

Luke waved to Carma and then maneuvered past the shoppers on the sidewalk toward his dad's shop. What was it about that boy, Howie wondered, that stirred his questions concerning faith? It seemed strange that such a quiet child could resurrect the struggle he had so forcefully put to rest. And yet, Howie realized, there was something more. For one moment, he had been privileged to see into an inquisitive, light-filled soul, and it had touched his heart with wonder.

When Luke entered the cobbler shop and disappeared from view, Howie ambled to the cherry wood desk and picked up a pencil and piece of paper. He hadn't written down a Wonder since—he couldn't even remember the last time—but now, he felt compelled to do so. He thought for several minutes, trying to put his feelings into a sentence. Finally, he wrote one word, *Luke*, and dropped it into Christmas Wonders.

He strode back to his office, determined to make a dent in the overflowing papers. After reading the same line umpteen times without clarity, he got up and took Lina's drawing from the shelf. His mind ran in a circle. Luke—the shepherds—Lina. Luke had said he would "go," and for some reason, Howie understood his simple commitment.

His mind settled on Lina and her pure faith. He had no doubt she, like Luke, would go if given the chance. But what would be the benefit? That question always caught him like a snare trap when he tried to reason through a step of faith. This time, however, he didn't turn away or bury the question in folds of forgetfulness. This time, he lifted his eyes to heaven and sought an answer.

And when he asked, the cobwebs of his mind cleared, and a pure light awakened his understanding. Only people like the shepherds, like Lina and Luke, who listened to the heavenly message and obeyed, could know—the Christ.

CHAPTER TEN

L uke threw his backpack over his shoulder, and flipped it around to catch it with his other arm. Resigned dread clouded his face. The only thing his classmates talked about was the upcoming Christmas holiday. Since he couldn't share in the excitement, he was excluded from their anticipation.

Even the snow, which fell for much of the previous week, dampened his spirits while it heightened the thrill that tingled among the other children. They talked with hope of getting new sleds, ice skates, and skis. Of course, the snow would make their perfect playground. For him, however, the snow and cold meant more time in their cramped apartment. He could do little outdoors on the city street in winter. In addition, the shops would be closed for several days. Since he and his dad were the only people who lived on the city block, they would be alone.

Luke collected his books that were due at the library, intent on asking for permission to check out a few extra books for the holiday. It would be something to pass the time.

He was preoccupied with plans and didn't realize his book bag had knocked his mother's picture off the small table until he heard the crash followed by the sound of breaking glass. "Oh, no!" he cried, falling to his knees.

His only treasure, the beautiful picture of his mother, was on the floor amongst shards of broken glass. That picture was entwined in every memory of his mother. It sustained him with recollections of warmth, of tenderness, of her.

After five years, it still reminded him of how it felt to crawl up on her bed and rest beside her, wrapped in her protecting arms. She sang to him on her "good days" when she could breathe without coughing after each word. On her "bad days," she just held him.

Most often, Luke and his mother were alone in the small cabin until darkness closed in around them. When Dad and Grandpa came home and prepared supper, Luke left his mother long enough to sit obediently at the table and eat. As soon as he was done, he ran back to his mother's side, never waiting for Dad who followed with her supper. Standing next to his mother's bed, he watched as Dad helped her sit with propped pillows to elevate her head. When she was comfortable, Dad encouraged her to eat.

Often, he took the spoon from her shaking hand, filled it with soup, and gently put it to her mouth, begging her to take one more bite.

After his mother had eaten, Luke took the dishes into the kitchen. Dad straightened the bed and helped her prepare for night. Usually, when Luke ran back into the bedroom, he found Dad holding his mother in his arms. Her frail body pressed firmly against his broad chest, her hand resting softly on his cheek.

One evening when Dad left the room, she lifted the picture from the bedside table and gave it to Luke. "I want you to have this."

Being so young, he didn't understand what she meant. When she fell asleep, he put it back in the accustomed place.

The next morning when she awoke and saw the picture on the table, she asked him to stand beside her bed. She picked up the picture, pressed it against his chest, and wrapped both of his arms around it. "Put this next to your bed so you'll see it every day. And remember me." A tender smile spread across her face in contrast to the tears that welled up in her eyes. "You're my treasure, Luke. I'll always watch over you, no matter where . . ."

As her voice choked off into a fit of coughing, Luke felt a warm, rushing sensation race along his arms and down his body. It was a feeling he wouldn't forget. In the years following her death, when he felt that sensation, he recalled her promise. He had come to believe she *was* watching over him, perhaps even guiding him from afar.

Luke was amazed to see his name in large print when Grandpa showed it to him in the Bible. When that feeling came, he felt the truth of Grandpa's words. Just last month, when he saw Christmas Wonders for the first time, that sensation alerted him to the importance of something he knew nothing about.

Perhaps, because of his need for comfort after breaking his treasure, that amazing, warm, rushing sensation spread through him as he picked up the broken frame. He looked down at the picture, relieved, but not surprised, to see it was unharmed. Eager to get the photograph away from the broken glass, he started to pull the back covering out of the frame. Then Dad called from the shop reminding him of the time. The clean-up project would have to wait until after school when he could do it carefully. He slipped the picture into his drawer, quickly swept the broken glass from the floor, grabbed his book bag, and headed to school.

———

At first, it seemed like any other school day as the students settled into their math and reading. But, to his surprise, it turned into an unusual day for he experienced feelings that were new to him. He couldn't really put a word to those feelings of disgust, embarrassment, and pleasure, but he felt each to the fullest.

The first obvious change occurred when his class went to the gym for recess. He was the first person knocked out of the dodgeball game. He clearly wasn't paying attention when the ball struck him, but he slumped to the ground, excluding himself from the next round of the game.

Later, Luke felt that annoying feeling of embarrassment. The feeling started when a girl walked by and dropped a small, ribbon-wrapped candy cane on his desk. When he tried to give it back, she refused to take it and said it was a Christmas gift. By the end of the school day, Luke had many treats and small wrapped gifts on his desk. He had nothing to give in return, so his embarrassment grew with each gift.

Finally, the day ended and all his classmates ran out in an expectant surge. Luke stood slowly, gathered up the library books that would mark his celebration, and turned to leave.

"Luke," Mrs. Layne called as she walked toward him. "Thanks for helping us look for Lina. We won't stop looking, will we?" Not waiting for an answer, she pointed to his desk. "Don't forget your presents."

"They're not mine."

"Oh? They're on your desk," she said. "I saw your friends give them to you."

"I didn't give them anything." He wanted to leave before he felt any more embarrassment.

Mrs. Layne walked across the room and picked up a

small sack. Returning to his desk, she put the gifts inside. "You know, gifts come in many different forms." She caught Luke's eye and tilted her head. "I don't think you realize what you've given us."

"Nothing," he blurted.

"You're wrong. That first day you came into class you gave me a very special gift."

"What?" Luke's eyes widened at the sharpness in his own voice.

She didn't seem to notice. "Until that day, most of the boys in our class didn't sit still and listen to me read. They'd make little noises with their feet or move their chairs and distract all the students around them. You came and seemed to enjoy my reading. It didn't take long before the other boys started acting like you."

Luke didn't have anything to say, so he just stared at his teacher, though a small smile turned up one side of his mouth.

Mrs. Layne sat down at one of the desks and motioned for Luke to sit beside her. "And you know, some of those same boys needed to be humbled a bit, and I've never thanked you for doing that as well."

Luke put his hand to his chest and shook his head. "I . . . I didn't do that."

"Oh yes, you did. It had been a long time since someone beat them at their own games, and you whipped them at dodgeball." She laughed softly. "And you're the one who helps Grace feel like part of the class by pushing her out for recess. Her mother said she's never felt so accepted." Mrs. Layne dabbed at her eyes.

"I better go, now." Luke pushed back his chair to stand, but Mrs. Layne put her hand on his arm.

Her eyes glistened and she drew in a deep breath. "And this quest to find Lina has made this season extra special." She smiled and raised her hand toward him as though saying *you're responsible for that as well*. "Then there was . . ."

By the time she finished telling him of the gifts he had given, the blush of embarrassment on his face had turned to a full, proud smile. He looked ready to burst with pleasure. Willingly he reached out his hand to accept the sack of gifts.

He was halfway down the hall before he realized there was one thing he could give in return. "Mrs. Layne," he called, running into his classroom, "I wish you a wonder-filled Christmas."

———

Luke sat on his bed, put the garbage can between his legs, and slowly pulled down the back of the broken frame as he watched the picture to make sure the glass pieces didn't cut it. He shook the frame gently, forcing the loose glass to fall into the garbage before turning it over to remove the picture. As he slid the back from the frame, he saw the edge of another paper where it bumped up against the picture.

He pulled out the paper and turned it over. Although he was totally focused on the picture, it took several minutes before he comprehended what he held in his hand. Even then, when he thought he had figured it out, he hesitated to believe it was real. Yet, somehow, he knew it had to be. Those eyes, that gentle smile, which always reached into his heart with a tender love, were the same. It was a picture of his mother as a child.

Setting the framed picture on his bed, he examined her hair, her face, and the tilt of her head. Though young, the eyes of the girl before him sparkled with life. He settled the picture over his heart as the feeling of pleasure swept through him for the second time in one day. His treasure had multiplied.

It was nearly impossible to keep his eyes off his mother's childhood photo as he cleaned out the frame and straightened up the older picture. When he was satisfied with his work, he put the framed picture back on the nightstand and propped the new one to the side so he could see both of them.

After checking for stray pieces of glass, he carried the garbage can outside to the trash. Task completed, he ran down the street toward the bookstore, hoping to make it inside before Carma closed for the night.

Luke hurried through the door, almost running into Carma.

"Whoa, Luke! What's going on?" She let out a startled laugh.

"I have a Christmas Wonder."

"I'm so glad. Go take care of that while I get the closed sign. I can't have any more customers tonight because we're having a party at my house and . . ." Carma kept talking about her plans as she put the sign on the door.

Luke ran to the cash register, picked up a paper, and wrote, *My mother's picture.* As he slipped it in Christmas Wonders, he looked up at Carma, and his eyes fairly danced. Then he grinned.

Carma stared at him. Her smile couldn't hide her look of surprise. "Wow," she laughed. "Can you tell me about it?"

"I found my mother's picture!" He sounded as though he had just won a grand prize.

"That's great. Where was it?"

Without hesitating, he told her the *entire* story of the hidden picture. "It's a Wonder, isn't it Carma?" he asked, his eyes begging for her approval.

Carma didn't answer for a minute. Her bottom lip quivered and she pressed both of her cheeks with her hands.

Luke watched her. "Carma?" he finally asked into the silence.

She held up one hand and coughed softly. "I think it's the most amazing Christmas Wonder I've ever heard about," she whispered in a quavering voice.

"You do?"

"Oh, yes. And I can't think of anyone else who deserves such an amazing Wonder." She put her hand to her forehead and looked down as her voice squeaked to a halt. With the shake of her head, she patted at her throat and drew in one long, deep breath. Her eyes rested on his face, a tender smile slid along her lips. "I'd like to see your pictures. I'll be here until noon tomorrow. Perhaps you could bring them over so I can—"

"They'd get wet."

"Hmm . . . if it's snowing. But I have waterproof envelopes. Why don't you take one? If you decide you'd like to bring the pictures with you tomorrow, they'll be all right." She opened the cupboard below the cash register, pulled out a large envelope, and handed it to Luke.

He reached out and wrapped his arms around her. "Thank you."

Carma held him tight until he loosened the hug, then she put her hands on his shoulders and looked into his joyful eyes. "Thank you, Luke. You've really given me something to think about this year and I want to . . ."

Although Carma didn't complete her sentence, Luke knew where her thoughts had strayed. For as they walked side by side to the front door, Carma talked about Christmas morning as though reviewing the list of program must-do's on him. She opened the door and paused as he stepped outside. "You and your dad are coming to the program. Aren't you?"

He shrugged.

"*You* want to come?"

He blinked. "Oh, yes."

"Hmm. Maybe if I talk to your dad . . ." She thought aloud as she closed the door behind him.

Carma stood by the window and watched Luke slip into the shadows of evening. When he was out of sight, she pulled the blind down and turned slowly away, bemused by the feelings he stirred in her heart.

CHAPTER ELEVEN

L uke pulled his mother's picture out of the broken frame and put it in the waterproof envelope alongside the picture he discovered the previous day. He stepped through the door from the apartment into the cobbler shop as a customer called out to Dad, "Have a wonder-filled Christmas."

Dad turned back to his worktable without responding. He didn't seem to notice the soft flakes of snow drifting down like a wish, nor Luke as he walked through the door to join the last minute shoppers on the busy sidewalk.

Opening his coat, Luke tucked the envelope inside and started toward the bookstore. He waved to Merv through the shoe store window and stopped to view the country village in the photographer's display case before picking up his pace.

Several customers milled around inside the bookstore. Carma was talking to a woman in the children's section. Luke strolled over to the hot chocolate dispenser, filled his cup with the rich liquid, and carried it to a reading table. After setting the cup down, he took a deep breath, filling his head with the sweet smell of chocolate. There was no reason to hurry.

He was just finishing the last drops in his cup when Carma stopped behind him and put her hand on his shoulder. "You brought the pictures." She slipped into the chair beside him with a long sigh.

Luke handed her the picture he found—his Christmas Wonder.

After only a glance at the black-and-white photograph, her questioning eyes shot back to Luke. "Your mother?" she said, holding the picture next to his face. "She seems . . . " She shook her head slightly. "It must be the eyes. They're so much like yours." Her gaze shifted between the picture and Luke several times before remaining on him. "I thought you looked like your dad, but now I see so much of your mother in you."

A customer walked into the store. Luke reached for the picture his mother had given him. "Here," he said, handing it to Carma. It wasn't that he didn't want to hear what Carma had to say about the picture of his mother as a child; he just knew she'd have to attend to her customer and he wanted her to see the woman he remembered.

Carma turned the picture away from the glare of the overhead light. "Oh, Luke," she whispered, "your mother was so beautiful. She has this glow that's just . . ." Carma put her hand to her chest and exhaled a short, broken sound.

Luke looked at her with grateful eyes.

Handing the pictures back to Luke, Carma glanced at a customer who set two books near the cash register. She frowned as she stood. "Luke, thank you for bringing your pictures. Now that I've seen her, I feel I know you a little better. I can't imagine how much you miss her." She held up one finger to the customer, and bent down eye to eye with Luke. "I want you to tell me about her. Let's talk after the holidays." Carma straightened, put on her working smile, and walked toward the cash register.

Luke watched her go, clinging to the pictures in his hands. He held up her pictures, studying one, then the other. "Oh Mother, help me," he whispered. "I don't want to forget you." When two more customers entered the shop, he slipped the pictures into the envelope to keep them dry on his way home.

———————

Throughout the morning, thoughts of Luke drifted through Carma's mind like the sun on a semi-cloudy day. When she told him about Christmas Wonders, she had no idea how his letter to Lina and *his* Wonders would touch her. Sometimes things happen that seem beyond the scope of coincidence. This was one of those times. Perhaps finding Lina would have brought it all together in a logical ending, but the journey itself had been a Wonder. She wanted to share that journey during her remembrance on the program, but she wasn't sure it was hers to share. What would Luke think? And would his dad approve? She needed to call Jeffrey and invite him to join them on Christmas morning—perhaps she would ask his permission to share the story of his son.

At noon, Carma turned the key in the lock and flipped off the lights in the front of the store. She went into her office and sat at her desk with a huge sigh of relief; the Christmas rush was over, at least the store's rush. Now, she had to get ready for her family's celebration and, of course, the Christmas Wonders Program.

She glanced through her mail for the last time before leaving the store, wishing for something that would cast a light on Lina's whereabouts. One of her tasks in their search had been to write the newspapers in the state. A number of them published her query, but she hadn't received anything in response. Still, she had hope; in fact, she believed that if she could share some current information about Lina, others in the community would join in the search. Perhaps in another year the founder of Christmas Wonders could attend the program.

Near the bottom of the pile, she saw a plain, white envelope with an unfamiliar return address. Her heart began to pound as she perused the short note. The letter was from a teacher who lived in a small town seven hours away. She taught a student named Lina Welton during her senior year, and, although they hadn't kept in touch, she saved her wedding announcement from the newspaper.

Great! Carma thought, her hopes soaring. That could provide a married name, the name of a spouse, parents, and perhaps even tell where they would live—what a boon that would be to their search. Maybe Luke's letter can be sent after all, and maybe next year . . . she smiled as she contemplated the possibility.

Returning to the envelope, Carma retrieved the strip of yellowed newspaper couched in front of the self-addressed envelope the woman had enclosed for the return of the article. She squealed as she read, "Audra and the late Benjamin Welton announce—" those were her parents! Then she saw *Lina* in quotation marks. Her jaw dropped and she laughed out loud. "Lina's a *nickname*," she whispered.

Chimes on her office clock intruded on her thoughts, bringing her back to the frustration of so much to do and so little time. She cast only a quick glance at the other names and details before tucking the announcement back in the envelope.

"Oh, Come All Ye Faithful," she started the carol, then hummed the tune as she gathered her office reports, purse, and coat. She plopped the letter on top of the stack.

With a quick turn of the key in her door, she put

business behind her and hurried to the car. When she dropped her armful onto the passenger seat, the letter slipped to the floor. Picking it up, she saw a small piece of newsprint which had edged out from behind the self-addressed envelope. Looking at the words, she figured Lina's teacher must have sent it to her by mistake.

However, when she turned the small clipping over, her astonished cry filled the air. It was a picture. Could it be? Was this beautiful woman really the little girl from long ago? It had to be the Lina they were looking for, and yet— she grabbed the newspaper announcement, searching for the information about the groom. *What was his name? Leonard . . . Leonard something,* she remembered when she glanced at it in her office. Now she read each sentence carefully. Her mind whirled. She sat back against the seat with a cry of bewilderment. Tears trickled down her face as she shook her head at the reality of their success.

CHAPTER TWELVE

The phone rang in the cobbler shop. Luke looked toward Dad's bedroom but didn't move from the old wooden rocker.

"Who would . . . ?" Dad's impatient mutter was lost in the creaking of his metal box springs. He trudged into the shop.

"Hello?" His voice was sharp.

"Who? Oh, yes." The one-sided conversation came through the open shop door; his voice was loud and clear to Luke.

"No," Dad said, tapping his knuckles on the counter. "Look, my wife died a week before Christmas. We have nothing to celebrate and I don't even want to . . ." He coughed.

Luke leaned back in his chair, returning his gaze to the library book with a sigh. Dad's voice was muffled by the tapping, which increased in volume and speed until . . . the tapping stopped.

Luke crept across the apartment to where he could see into the shop. Dad stared out the front window. He held the phone with one hand and his other hand was in front of him, clenched into a fist.

"I don't think so." He shook his head, leaned against the counter, and dropped his hand as though its weight was unmanageable. After another pause, he said in a slow, strained voice, "Why would I say anything?"

Hurrying back to his chair, Luke picked up his book and held it in front of his face, acting as though he hadn't been eavesdropping. When Dad didn't come back into the apartment after abruptly hanging up the phone, Luke figured he must have found work that needed his attention. Luke read twenty pages before Dad's footsteps pattered into the apartment and then stopped just inside the doorway.

After several minutes, Dad took a few steps and stopped again. Repeating the pattern, he made his way into the kitchen, stopped, and just looked around as if he were confused. Without glancing at Luke, he walked to the back door, opened it, and stood in the doorway, turning his head right then left, right then left. Finally, he closed the door and shuffled to the kitchen window. Once again, he glanced around, his eyes settling on different places inside and outside of the room.

When he noticed Luke, he jerked back, his eyes bulging. "Uhh . . . Carma said you found a picture of your mother," he stammered, his voice barely recognizable.

"I'm sorry, I broke—"

"No." Dad held up his hand. "You found her picture. May I see it?"

Luke dashed to his room and returned with the envelope, the two pictures still inside. Dad took it from his outstretched hand, turned, and walked away.

Sitting back in the chair, Luke picked up the book and tried to read, but he couldn't pay attention. Questions popped in his head like corn in a hot skillet. *Why was Dad acting so strange? Was he mad about the picture frame? What did he think about the picture? Did Carma invite him to the program? When he said no on the telephone, was that his answer to Carma's invitation?*

Finally, Luke gave up on the book, ate a bowl of cereal, and crawled into bed. Although it was Christmas Eve, he didn't lie awake with excitement awaiting the early light of Christmas morning. He had no recollection of a celebration to stir embers of hope and anticipation. It would be just another day.

━━━━━━━━━━

Sometime in the night, Luke awoke and saw the light in Dad's room. He slipped out of bed and shuffled to the door. Dad was bent over the desk in the corner of the room, his head resting on his arms. Scattered papers cluttered the desk and surrounding floor. The pictures leaned against the wall.

Luke almost put his hand on Dad's shoulder to wake him so he could get into bed. Instead, he turned off the light, returned to his own room, and once again crawled under the covers.

━━━━━━━━━━

When Luke awoke on Christmas morning, he lay still for several minutes. A whole day with nothing to do stretched in front of him like an empty memory. Finally, he got up and slipped on his shirt and pants. Some of the boys at school were thrilled about having nothing to do for a whole week, but Luke didn't "do nothing" well, not even for a day.

While making his bed, he was startled by a knock on the back door of their apartment. It wasn't a quiet I'm-here-sorry-to-disturb-you knock, but rather it was a loud, insistent blow. Water, hitting the sides of the old shower, let him know Dad wasn't going to answer the door. Nobody had come to that door since he and Dad moved to the city. Why would someone come now?

The volume of knocking increased as Luke trudged from his bedroom and across their small kitchen. He looked out the window before unlocking the door. Nan stood outside, her hands full. She kicked the door again before noticing him. "Hi, Nan what . . .?" He jumped back as Nan pushed past him into the apartment without waiting for an invitation.

"Merry Christmas, Luke. You never came over for a cinnamon roll so I brought you some." She set the plate of rolls on the counter. "And this," she said, holding up a thermos, "is warm wassail, our traditional Christmas drink."

"Thanks. Those cinnamon rolls look—"

"Hey, what's all that?" Nan asked, pointing across the room.

The table and surrounding floor were covered with papers, envelopes, and half-emptied boxes. "I don't know." He stepped toward the piles.

"I wanted to get here earlier so we could have a roll and wassail before going to the program, but I got delayed with phone calls and presents and—"

"Nan?" Dad stopped mid-step.

"Sorry to startle you." She laughed but didn't comment on his open shirt and towel sharpened hair. "Just brought you a cinnamon roll and wassail for your Christmas breakfast." She glanced at her watch. "But it'll have to wait until after the program. We've got to get going or we'll be late."

"We're not going."

"Why?" Red Christmas bulbs on Nan's ear lobes jiggled as she shook her head.

"We don't celebrate Christmas, and besides, I've got work to do." Dad waved toward the piles of papers.

"Oh, come on, Jeffrey. You're a part of this community. Don't act so—"

"No!" Dad said, stepping back. He winced, as if he had surprised himself with his harsh behavior. With barely a pause, he spoke in a subdued tone. "I really appreciate what you've done for us, it's just that Christmas is full of . . . of memories I choose to forget."

Nan turned toward the door as though she were going to leave without responding. Luke's hope vanished with her back until she looked over her shoulder at him and jerked her head. "Come on, Luke, I don't want to go alone."

Luke stepped toward Dad, his eyes bright as he asked, "May I?"

Dad's eyebrows pinched together. He started to speak and then stopped. With a flip of his hand, he turned abruptly and walked into the bedroom.

When the door was firmly shut behind them, Nan shook her head and muttered, "Oh my." Turning to Luke with a forced smile, she added, "I'm glad you're coming with me," before setting the pace for a brisk walk.

A few cars were parked along their street, but it wasn't until they reached the corner that they saw a steady stream of people moving toward the community building. Luke waved to one of his classmates who called out a Christmas greeting and waited beside Nan as she talked with a man Luke didn't know. After a startled glance at her watch, she led the way up the steps and into the old stone building.

Music from the grand pipe organ greeted them as they slid into a bench on the outside aisle. Luke looked around in awe. It seemed like a perfect place for a Christmas cel-ebration. Stained-glass windows depicted the Christmas story. The old community center was one of the first churches in the area. When it was no longer feasible to use it as a church, volunteers had raised money to buy it for a community hall.

Luke looked from window to window, pausing for a minute on the shepherds, not so very different from Lina's drawing. Thinking back on the search for her, he was disappointed at their failure. Yet, due to the search, Christmas Wonders was now a part of his life. Still, he wished Lina could be here for the program; she should see the impact of her simple gift in the lives of so many people.

His eyes skipped to the front of the hall where Joseph, Mary, and the baby Jesus huddled together in the stable. Morning sun shone radiantly through the pane, casting ripples of colored light across the audience. Luke gazed at the crowd. The light of His love radiated on the face of each person—the same light Luke had seen when Merv shared Lina's letter.

When the mayor stood to welcome the crowd, Luke continued to follow the rays of light. However, when Carma went to the microphone and announced the speakers, Luke turned his attention to the program. Before long, he was listening intently. Three people shared their Christmas Wonders. Two of the people knew Lina and mentioned her by name. They told how a Wonder made a significant difference in their lives; it was easy to see why they loved Christmas Wonders.

After their comments, organ music once again filled the air. The crowd stood to sing. Part way through the song, Nan pulled on Luke's arm and motioned toward the door. "Let's slide over for your dad."

Dad strode along the back of the room. Before moving up the aisle to where he and Nan stood, Dad stopped and looked toward the podium. He was still standing there when the music ended. Everyone else in the room sat. Dad took a few steps forward and nodded as though communicating with someone in front of the room. He paused again, eyes focused on the podium. Then, with his head bent, he slid into the seat next to Luke.

It was Carma's turn to speak. She adjusted the microphone, but instead of beginning, she paused for several moments looking out at the gathered crowd. She coughed quietly, clearing her throat, and gazed right at Luke. When she smiled, Luke nodded at her, acknowledging across the crowded space that her smile was meant just for him. When she asked for everyone who had experienced a Christmas Wonder to raise a hand, all the people Luke could see, besides Dad, responded.

Carma took her time scanning the crowd before announcing triumphantly, "We are almost totally united in a Wonder. For those of you who didn't raise your hand," she said softly, then her volume increased with a tone of conviction, "Today, you *will* experience a Christmas Wonder."

Stiffening, Dad leaned forward. His jaw was rigid, hands clenched on his thighs and his feet were planted on the floor as though preparing for escape.

Carma explained about the beginning of their tradition as she told of the little girl, who, through her simple gifts, had been an inspiration to their street and city. She told of Luke's suggestion that they invite Lina to join in their celebration and the resulting search for the founder of Christmas Wonders.

A ripple of excitement spread through the crowd when she spoke of their quest. As she thanked all those who assisted in the search, her voice dropped to a whisper and then faded into silence.

The feeling of anxious expectancy hung in the room like a mysterious summons. Nobody moved or made a sound.

Carma put her hand to her mouth and shut her eyes. When at last she opened them, she attempted to smile through quivering lips. The microphone flashed with static as she gulped in forced breaths. She braced herself on the podium and began to speak as though she were a reporter relaying a news event. "I'm sorry to report that our dear Lina passed away some years ago."

A collective gasp broke from the crowd. People turned to their neighbors to express their common sorrow. Luke looked straight ahead, but something collapsed in his eyes. Lina's legacy had touched him with a kindness and understanding that reached out silently through the years. This was not what he expected from a program to celebrate Christmas Wonders. Instead of a celebration, it seemed like a funeral, an event too familiar in his young life.

As confusion rippled through the crowd, something touched his shoulder. Luke turned toward the touch. Dad's long arm lay across his back. It was such an unfamiliar connection. Giving way to the pressure of Dad's hand, Luke slid under the protecting comfort of his arm, his eyes lifting to Dad's face. Sorrow, long hidden, shaded Dad's troubled eyes.

At Carma's request, the crowd quieted for a minute of silence to remember Lina. An expectant desire shifted through the crowd when they opened their eyes and looked toward the podium. Surely, there had to be something that would lift their hearts. After all, Carma promised them a Christmas Wonder.

"I, like you, felt that sorrow when I learned of Lina's death. Many of you will continue to mourn for her as I will. But I believe today you'll see a Christmas Wonder to share with your loved ones for many years to come.

"Christmas Wonders has been a special part of my celebration since I was in college. I have enjoyed the fun, creative aspects of the season and felt as though those things were the most important elements of Christmas. This year, however, our street was once again blessed with a child when Luke moved into the apartment where Lina lived. Through his eyes, I saw Christmas Wonders that touched my heart with understanding of the *true* wonder of our Savior's love. I find it amazing *he* was the one who initiated our quest to find Lina.

"It was not until yesterday that I learned Lina's name was actually Evangelina. Most of us still think of her as a little girl. But she grew up, married, and had a son. Today, it is our privilege to have her husband and son with us. After we sing 'Silent Night,' I know you'll welcome them with the same warmth you'd show her."

Although everyone was still listening intently to Carma, people in the crowd turned in their seats, searching for two unfamiliar faces. Luke sat still. Most of the people around him were strangers; he wouldn't know if someone new was among them. Besides, it had been years since he felt Dad's arm around his shoulders.

Carma paused once again. Unembarrassed, she wiped at her eyes while waiting for the audience to complete their scan of the crowd and return their attention to her. Across the electrified audience, she caught Luke's gaze, smiled tremulously at him, and whispered, "We welcome Lina's husband, Leonard Jeffrey Cardston, and her *son*, Luke."

CHAPTER THIRTEEN

I f someone had asked Luke about his feelings, it would have been impossible for him to describe them. Everything about Lina amazed him, but the stories were of a girl, close to his age. There was no way, during those moments of such intense shock, he could fit what he knew of Lina into *his* memory of *his* mother. They were two separate individuals. How could they be the same person?

He didn't have long to connect his knowledge with his memory because Nan flipped around, her jaw hung loose, her eyes round as a harvest moon. "Why didn't you tell me? I can't believe this. It's . . . it's incredible!" The hand she rested on Luke's arm trembled. "Lina's son. I'm just . . ."

Luke didn't hear the rest of her astonishment, because the meeting ended and he and Dad were surrounded by a crowd. Many of them wanted to share their personal memories of his mother. Others just wanted to exclaim over their surprise.

Donna almost climbed over the bleachers in her attempt to ask the obvious question. "Why didn't you tell us you were Lina's son?" She blurted before actually reaching him.

Shrugging his shoulders was Luke's only response. He didn't have answers, just plenty of questions. When Carma started down the aisle of the community center, he slipped away from Dad and the people gathered around them.

Just before Luke reached Carma, Merv stepped up and took both of them by the arm. "You're sure about this, Carma?"

"Yes," she said on a deep exhale.

"Carma?" Luke touched her hand. "How—"

"Oh, Luke." Carma put her other hand on Luke's shoulder, and searched his face with gentle, moist-filled eyes. "This has been so amazing; a Wonder I'll never forget. I told you I was going to send letters to newspapers. I hoped they'd do us a favor by helping to find Lina. It seemed like wasted effort—until yesterday. One of her teachers sent me your parents' wedding announcement. And you know that picture you showed me of your mother?"

"The one I found?"

"No, the other one. It was in the newspaper!"

Luke gulped. "My mother's . . ." Retracing the series of events, he couldn't quite connect the steps that led to this moment.

"He showed you her picture?" Merv asked, his eyes shifting back and forth between Luke and Carma. "And that's how you tied this all together?"

Carma held up both hands. "It was all there in the wedding announcement. Still, I wasn't certain. There wasn't any proof that Luke's mother lived here when she was young, until . . ." She leaned toward Luke, her eyes intent. "Your dad came in and nodded to me. He must have found something that placed her here as a child."

"My dad?" Luke shook his head. "Why didn't he tell me?"

"He had no idea until I called him."

"Last night?"

Dad's unusual behavior of the previous evening suddenly made sense. No wonder he walked around their apartment looking at it as though he'd never seen it; he never had seen it in relation to his mother.

"It was a shock to him." Carma laughed. "Poor man." She covered her mouth, but her eyes were sharp with the smile she tried to hide.

"But . . . but did he even know about Christmas Wonders?" Merv asked.

Carma glanced at Merv, eyebrows raised. "We didn't really get into that." Her eyes returned to Luke. "It's gotta be hard for him to realize so many of us knew her. Of course, he wouldn't believe it just because of the letter." Her eyes skimmed over the crowd until they rested on Dad. "I bet he was awake half the night trying to verify a connection."

"There were papers all over." Luke glanced at Dad and muttered, "What did he find?"

————————

Luke skipped down the stairs of the old stone building. Everything looked the same, but everything felt different somehow. It was like coming back to a place you belonged, a place of comfort. He glanced around, dazed. This was the very place his mother had known and obviously loved as a child. This was home. Perhaps it was her sense of belonging that filled him with his own feeling of home.

He and Dad crossed the street and turned the corner by the drug store. Dad stopped, his gaze intent on something in the display window. Luke followed his gaze. Christmas Wonders was in the middle of the Christmas scene. Donna must have put it there after closing the store on Christmas Eve.

"Is that what everyone was talking about?" Dad asked.

Luke nodded.

Dad didn't say anything more about Christmas Wonders in the window of Nan's Diner, the photography shop, and the shoe store, but Luke stopped beside him in front of each one. To a stranger, the package wrapped in paper with musical notes, harps, and angels in long, flowing gowns may appear of little worth beside the more costly, purchased decorations, but each one was the very heart of Christmas.

When they reached their apartment, instead of going

directly to his bedroom as Luke expected, Dad walked to the corner of the kitchen where a row of unpacked boxes still lined the wall. He began shuffling the boxes around. Luke crossed his arms and rubbed his hands up and down the prickles which erupted like goose bumps in a full body surge.

Dad set a box on the table, pulled open the flaps, and reached inside. "Evangelina's . . . how did this . . .?" He tossed a book on the table.

Luke leapt toward it.

"Your grandpa must have put it—"

"Mother's Bible," Luke whispered, lifting the book from the table. He held it to his chest. His mother's treasure lost—now found. The radiating warmth that raced along his skin tingled inside.

"I think it's here somewhere." Dad pulled objects from the box and set them on the table: a folded linen cloth with red flowers on a green background, a box of small, white bells, and a beautiful angel, her halo slightly askew.

Luke's heart pounded. The warm, rushing sensation throbbed along his flesh like a wave on sun-drenched sand. Suddenly, Dad stood straight, his eyes riveted into the interior. Then, dropping his hands to his side, he backed away from the box, shaking his head as though trying to rid it of some unseen demon.

Setting the Bible next to the angel, Luke jumped on the chair and peered inside the box. He gulped in a whoosh of air. "Dad!" he cried, recognizing the corner of a package.

Could it really be? Had it been there all these years, forgotten and unused?

Tenderly, he reached into the box and freed *her* Christmas Wonders from a strand of bubble lights. Lifting it like a priceless gift, he cradled it in his arms. Over the past month, he had learned about the little girl who started Christmas Wonders through the memories of others. Perhaps now, through her Wonders, he could learn about his mother.

As he started to lift the top off her Wonders, he noticed Dad, standing like a statue. Luke extended the treasure toward him. "Here, Dad," he said, "You open it."

Dad glanced at Evangelina's Christmas Wonders, arms still stiff at his side. Taking a step back, he stared at Luke, his eyes dark with alarm.

"Please?" Luke pressed Dad's hand with the package.

Dad backed away. The look on his face shifted from alarm to something Luke had never seen before. "Your mother left it for you," he said, his voice taut.

Without another word, Dad turned and walked toward his bedroom. Luke pulled the treasure into the cradling protection of his arms as he watched his dad's back.

━━━━━━━━━

Although he maintained some semblance of composure until he slipped into the privacy of his bedroom, Dad had to get away from Evangelina's Christmas Wonders. He braced himself against the wall. His chest constricted, forcing him to take panting breaths. Then he lost control of his spiraling emotions.

Five years ago, after burying the love of his life, he had thrown all her Christmas treasures into a box. He should have gotten rid of them, and probably would have if there had been time to sort through the old stuff in the attic before moving. Without her, there was no reason to think about the holidays. And yet, after being subjected to a remembrance for his wife, and then seeing Christmas Wonders in the display windows, he had hurried home and searched for that very box. Lina's reading award from Luke's school verified his wife had once lived in town, but he needed more. He had to know if everyone's claim of relationship to her was real. If her Christmas Wonders matched those in the town, the connection would be unquestionable.

But in his hurry, he hadn't even considered what her Wonders could mean to Luke, until it was too late. Luke acted as though finding Evangelina's Christmas Wonders was akin to discovering a buried treasure. But the wrapped package which Luke held with amazed joy was as threatening to Dad as a coyote to newborn lambs. It contained her feelings, her hopes, her Wonders—and, long ago, he had built a wall around his heart to keep those things out.

A barrage of memories flooded his brain, threatening to wreak havoc on his self-imposed stoicism. Thoughts of Evangelina—eyes glowing with the delight of Christmas, pressed upon him. For years, she had tried to persuade him to share a Wonder. There was something almost magical about watching her find pleasure in their simple life, but he had been too busy, distracted, or perhaps just unwilling to see past the difficulties of their existence.

His knees threatened to collapse under the weight of recollections. He staggered to the chair, needing to get away from everything that used to be. But Evangelina's eyes met him in duplicate—soft, beautiful, accusing. He knocked the picture of Evangelina as a child face down on the desk. His desire to keep every memory of her alive warred with his determination to bury them. He choked on a wave of pain. After dropping his head down, he was unaware of the second picture that fell against his hair.

When his heart returned to the slow, smooth rhythm of control, he lifted his head. The picture fell onto the pile of papers. Shocked at having caused both pictures to be hidden from view, he quickly retrieved them. After glancing at each one, he pressed his eyes shut, but the image of her remained. He shook his head, fully aware of his futile attempt to dislodge the memories. But the pictures? At least he could get them out of his sight. He pushed his chair away from the desk.

Flashes of colored light hit the walls and ceiling of the kitchen. Dad paused and stared at the table, now covered with Evangelina's green linen cloth. In the center, Christmas Wonders was flanked on either side by the angel and the figurine of Mary holding the baby Jesus. Evangelina's Bible, artistically draped with a soft white cloth, sat in front, and the bubble lights encircled the table—a Christmas oasis in the midst of a desert of forgotten hope.

He stopped, and then took a step back. How could he find rest from her memory when Luke was so much like her? With a clenched fist, he forced himself forward and set the pictures on the table.

"Dad." Luke caught his hand before he could escape. "This is for you." He thrust a white slip of paper toward him.

Reaching out reluctantly, he glanced at Evangelina's writing. *Jeffrey, my love*—the phrase shot like a bolt of lightning through his body as Evangelina's voice repeated those words in his mind. That was her favorite expression for him, and at one point he was almost unaffected by it. But now?

"Here." Luke held out another paper.

Jeffrey holding our sleeping son. His hand flew to his chest and he drew in a sharp breath. Her words, her voice brought those moments of long ago to the present and he could feel how he felt then. He heard the sound of her laughter as she watched him run into the bedroom and pick up their sleeping son. She never scolded him, at least not that he could remember, and now he knew why. To her, his love was a Wonder.

Luke touched his arm. He jumped. He'd been so

caught up in memories of her; he had almost forgotten he wasn't alone. But the look of tender longing in Luke's eyes brought him back to reality as quickly as his question. "Did you really?"

After giving only a nod in response, he realized his son, *their* son, really didn't know. How could he? Seeped in his own misery and disappointments, he had turned his back on Evangelina's son—the child she had been willing to die for, but for whom she had longed to live.

"Luke, I'm so . . . so sorry," Dad cried as he reached out and pulled Luke to his chest. Years of suppressed feelings soared to life, swirling inside of him like a life-giving storm in the mountains.

When Luke looked at Dad, his eyes were as bright as the bubble lights. With Dad's arm still around his shoulders, he pointed at his mother's treasure and said with the conviction of understanding, "Her Christmas Wonders are for *us*!"

Dad's mouth trembled. He pressed his eyes with his fingers and gulped in a stream of deep breaths. When he looked back at Luke, his eyes shone with a tender warmth and he whispered, "You're right."

Luke smiled like a boy on Christmas morning as one by one *her* Christmas Wonders of the past became *their* Christmas Wonders of the present.

Reading the Bible with Jeffrey

Snow-frosted trees

Luke's laughter

Meeting Jeffrey under the mistletoe

Snuggling with Luke

Finding the perfect Christmas tree

Singing the Silent Night lullaby

Luke's reverence when he looks at my Nativity

Walking through the snow with Jeffrey

Waking up Christmas morning

The smell of Dad's cooking

Christmas Wonders

Christmas Wonders

Robyn Buttars

ABOUT THE AUTHOR

ROBYN BUTTARS is an award-winning author of books for children and adults. Her first novella, *Christmas Rose*, won first place in the League of Utah Writer's Contest and was a holiday bestseller. Her home is Lewiston, Utah, and she and her husband, Kent, are the parents of six children. She is a registered nurse and enjoys traveling, composing, and reading.

ABOUT FAMILIUS

Welcome to a place where parents are celebrated, not compared. Where heart is at the center of our families, and family at the center of our homes. Where boo-boos are still kissed, cake beaters are still licked, and mistakes are still okay. Welcome to a place where books—and family—are beautiful. Familius: a book publisher dedicated to helping families be happy.

Visit Our Website: www.familius.com

Our website is a different kind of place. Get inspired, read articles, discover books, watch videos, connect with our family experts, download books and apps and audiobooks, and along the way, discover how values and happy family life go together.

Join Our Family

There are lots of ways to connect with us! Subscribe to our newsletters at www.familius.com to receive uplifting daily inspiration, essays from our Pater Familius, a free ebook every month, and the first word on special discounts and Familius news.

Become an Expert

Familius authors and other established writers interested in helping families be happy are invited to join our family and contribute online content. If you have something important to say on the family, join our expert community by applying at:

www.familius.com/apply-to-become-a-familius-expert

Get Bulk Discounts

If you feel a few friends and family might benefit from what you've read, let us know and we'll be happy to provide you with quantity discounts. Simply email us at specialorders@familius.com.

Website: www.familius.com

Facebook: www.facebook.com/paterfamilius

Twitter: @familiustalk, @paterfamilius1

Pinterest: www.pinterest.com/familius

The most important work

you ever do will be within the

walls of your own home.